Marjorie Darke

A LONG WAY TO GO

PUFFIN BOOKS

Puffin Books, Penguin Books Ltd, Harmondsworth, Middlesex, England
Viking Penguin Inc., 40 West 23rd Street, New York, New York 10010, U.S.A.
Penguin Books Australia Ltd, Ringwood, Victoria, Australia
Penguin Books Canada Limited, 2801 John Street, Markham, Ontario, Canada L3R 1B4
Penguin Books (N.Z.) Ltd, 182–190 Wairau Road, Auckland 10, New Zealand

First published by Kestrel Books 1978
Published by Puffin Books 1982
Reprinted 1984, 1986

Made and printed in Great Britain by
Hazell Watson & Viney Limited,
Member of the BPCC Group,
Aylesbury, Bucks

PUFFIN PLUS

A LONG WAY TO GO

London during the First World War, and all over the city the posters are screaming at Luke: YOUR COUNTRY NEEDS YOU! The trouble is, he just doesn't want to fight, however much his twin sister Bella and his grandfather urge him on. Then he comes across Stan, who has no intention of fighting and is on the run from the police and the army. Could Luke do the same?

A Long Way to Go is the story of one boy's struggle for what he believes to be right, with all the characters who help to shape his future. In particular, there's the marvellous figure of Bella, desperately close to Luke yet unable to understand his feelings when she herself is full of frustration at only being allowed to work in a munitions factory.

This is a vivid story of a city at war and it strikingly conveys the tensions and feelings of the times.

Marjorie Darke was born in Birmingham and educated in Worcester. She attended the Leicester College of Art and the Central School of Art, then worked as a textile designer for some years. She is married to an artist and has three grown-up children. Marjorie Darke lives in Somerset.

Other books by Marjorie Darke

COMEBACK
THE FIRST OF MIDNIGHT
MESSAGES:
A collection of shivery tales

1

THE train whistle shrieked twice.

'I'm off then, Bella.'

Pressurized steam jetted from the safety valve, roaring up into the girdered roof of Victoria Station.

'Tata, our Jack.'

From the end of the platform a crabbed old porter in a buttoned-up jacket was beginning to limp the length of the train, urging reluctant Tommies to climb aboard. Slamming doors like doom.

'See after the Admiral and our Luke, and write to us. You will write?'

There was a wistful note in her brother's voice that cut her to the heart and brought embarrassment. Big bluff Jack Knight, promising middleweight, hard as nails, selfish as they come, appealing to *her*!

'Course! And don't you fret about nothink. I'll keep me eye on things. Shan't let our Luke have it all his own way!'

He laughed. A brittle sound, but still a laugh. It pushed back her lurking suspicion that he didn't want to go to war, might even be *afraid*. The idea was smothered as he loomed over her. A crippling hug knocked her hat over one ear and a smacking kiss on each cheek sent it slithering backwards.

'Yer a grand girl, Bella. Ain't no flies on you,' he said and swung the kit-bag on to his broad shoulder, stepping up into the train. 'Shove over, Pozzo, make some room can't you? Blimey it's packed tighter than the Feathers on a Saturday night!'

The oily smell of khaki cloth was in her nostrils, astonishment in her mind. Through a wavering mist she saw the light-brown skin of his neck and hands, but quickly rubbed her eyes before he could turn and guess her true feelings.

'YOUR COUNTRY NEEDS YOU!' the poster told her; Kitchener's finger, which would have pointed straight at her, was hidden by a tall man in the uniform of an officer in the Royal Flying Corps. He stood close to the stocky girl with the apple cheeks and flyaway hair who had knocked against her at the barrier. A country girl. More at home in green lanes than here. They'd exchanged smiles, separated, and now come together again. Bella watched, held by a tension she could almost see, it was so apparent. Man and girl neither touched nor spoke, but read each other's faces as if it was the end of the world. Then the girl fumbled in her pocket, dragged something out and dropped it. Both went down together, bumping shoulders, and came up laughing – the girl with wet cheeks. The airman grabbed her hand, and they were lost from sight behind the moving crowd of mothers, sisters, sweethearts, wives, who jostled for better positions at the open carriage windows.

'Bel*la*!'

She'd been divided from the train without noticing and pushed towards the carriage door and Jack's grimly cheerful face. There was a nightmare feel to this day. She didn't want to be here. Perhaps she'd wake soon and find a normal spud-peeling fire-making Chrisp Street Market Saturday, with the Admiral nodding in his rocking chair. She smiled in an effort to act normally, wriggling towards him.

'Cor what a crush!'

'All London come to see me off,' he said and winked. 'Nice to be so popular. It's being so handsome as does it. Draws 'em like pins to a magnet.'

'Taking yer trumpet along, that's for sure,' she said, trying to be equally chirpy.

A round face splodged with freckles, khaki cap stuck on the back of ginger curls, peered over the breadth of Jack's shoulder. 'He can't wait to try his charms on them French mademysells, can y'Jack? Thinks they'll come flocking.'

'Oh he fancies himself as a ladykiller – no need to tell me. I've lived with him all me life,' Bella said.

Jack put a large brown hand over the freckles and gave a friendly shove. 'Gerron with you, Pozzo! You ain't no monk.' He turned back, his face cracking into a set grin. 'Nothink like a holiday in gay Paree.'

A *holiday*!

The guard's whistle shrilled. The train jerked. Bodies crammed closer in last farewells. The crowd pushed, shoved, parted enough for Bella to catch a quick glimpse of the airman as he grabbed the handle of a first-class compartment, opened the door and heaved himself into the crawling train. From somewhere down the platform a strong contralto voice began singing:

'Rule Britannia, Britannia rules the waves,
Britons never never never shall be slaves ...'

The sound was caught up, swelling into a ragged choir as the train lurched, then moved steadily. All the windows were packed with waving khaki arms and the white discs of faces blurring into nonentity. Blurring even more, because try as she would, Bella couldn't get her popping emotions to behave. She tried to pick out Jack, but couldn't – his brown skin had merged with khaki and carriage door. Oh it wasn't fair ... it wasn't fair! The clacking train wheels made a rhythm of her thoughts. It wasn't fair ... it wasn't fair! She wanted to find a hole where she could bury her head and have a good roar with nobody to watch. Jack gone. Luke next. While she ... But what if it had been Luke this time? She backed off from the idea. Take care of that when it happened, as it inevitably would, unless the war was over by Christmas. People said it would be. They'd said the same thing last year. Injustice hit her, coupling with a heart-leap of real fear for her beloved Luke. She swivelled away from the platform edge and was face to face with the country girl who was easing through the crowd as she scrubbed her nose like a kitchen floor.

'Grim ain't it?' Bella said on impulse.

'Yo can say that again!' the girl replied, muffled in handkerchief, destroying her country connections with a sing-song Birmingham accent. She blew her nose loud and hard, then put the handkerchief firmly back in her pocket. 'Let's get out of here. I hate good-byes.'

There was that smile again, crooked and warming; full of humour.

'Me too.'

They struggled through the spreading crush, through the barrier, through the booking hall and into thin cool street drizzle which earlier had drowned the July sun and now was allowing watery light to trickle between parted clouds.

They hesitated on the pavement, flat and purposeless now that the train had gone. There was nothing to keep them.

'Yo been on this caper before?' the girl asked, dawdling.

'No. Me brother's not long volunteered.' The oddity of this fact, laid alongside the strong feeling she'd had that Jack wished he was anywhere but on the train heading for the trenches, came with force. She drew in her breath sharply.

'I *know*!' The girl took Bella's hand and squeezed it sympathetically.

'You don't.'

'But I do. It's my second time and it don't get any better.'

The misunderstanding was complete and, slightly ashamed, Bella said: 'It ain't what you thinks. Course I'm sorry to see him go.' Was she? They'd never been close. Not like it was with Luke. 'I don't want him to get hurt or killed.' Truth there. 'But ... well, you don't know how I wish it was me on that train.'

The girl released her hand and stared.

Bella rushed on: 'What is there to *do*? 'Cept sit at home and sew ruddy buttons on shirts and knit balaclavas. Not to mention socks – never can get the perishers to end up the same length! I can't even get a job. There ain't much our way and I can't leave home because of the Admiral.'

'The Admiral?'

Bella looked down at the chocolate skin of her hand that still retained the warm pressure, slowly turning it over, pink palm upwards. She said absently: 'No big brass. Just a nickname for me Grandad on account of him being christened Horatio Nelson,' her mind drifting back inexorably to the enigma of Luke who came and went in the house now as if it was only the shell of himself who was there.

They stood under the protection of the station canopy, still held together by the last invisible threads of shared experience; reluctant to take up the routines of ordinary life again. And into the pause came the crisp hard sound of marching feet. Together they looked towards the top of the street and saw the head of a platoon of kilted soldiers rounding the corner. In full pack and led by a piper, they marched with a swing as if glad to be on the move; faces fresh and wind weathered. Watching, Bella felt an upsurge of envy, laced with powerful tingling excitement which filled her throat and misted her eyes.

'Poor devils.'

Shocked, Bella said: 'Lucky, you means.'

'Depends on your point of view.' There was an edge of irony to the girl's voice which left Bella puzzled.

'You ain't *against* them, surely?'

'Oh not the lads. They're grand. Every one. But I hates this war. It's cruel and stupid. A lot of blockheads telling everyone else what to do. Makes fools of us all.'

'You shouldn't think like that. You shouldn't say such things. We're all in this together. Talking like that's the way to *lose*. It's ... it's like burning the flag!'

The girl shrugged. 'No offence, love, but I ain't got them sort of patriotic feelings.'

'But we're right and they're wrong, know what I means?' Bella insisted. 'Course, no one *wants* war.'

'Don't they? I ain't so sure about that.'

'No ... course they don't. But it's here and we've got to give 'em a walloping. Put our backs into it and *win*. That's what I believes.'

'I can't help the way I feels.' The girl was apologetic. 'It's seeing me friend off, I suppose. My brother's out in France an' all. Screws me up inside thinking – they could die.'

Bella's indignation turned to compassion. 'At least if they did you could be proud, couldn't you? Knowing they'd died for their country. They'd be real heroes. If it happens to our Jack . . . and please Gawd it won't . . . I know I'd feel like that.'

'Yo can't believe what yo're saying?'

I've shocked her, Bella thought – we've shocked each other. She said emphatically: 'I mean every word.'

The girl waved her hand towards the soldiers who had been halted at the entrance to the station.

'You wants to ask 'em,' Bella said before she could say anything. 'They're glad to be going. Proud. Bet you a tanner to a florin!'

As if saluting her faith in them the piper began inflating the bag of his pipes with strong breath; the first droning sounds rising into a penetrating reedy melody that lifted her heart and set her feet tapping. Oh she was right . . . right! She felt exultant.

Over the top of the music, barked commands brought the soldiers to smart attention and sent them wheeling right to march briskly through into the station.

Stirred almost to tears, Bella watched them go. Even the plaguing thought – what if it had been Luke on his way to France? – had lost its power. The soldiers were gone but the music still echoed plaintively into the pale sunlight, plucking at her heartstrings. How brave they were! How courageous! Full to overflowing, she turned round, sure that these sentiments must be shared; wanting to have her ruffled feelings lulled back into security. But in that brief moment the girl had gone.

For no reason she could understand, Bella felt absurdly let down. In place of her high excitement was the familiar rising tide of nameless fear which always lurked, waiting to pounce when she least expected. She never even told me her name, she thought, and examined the brown skin of her hands for a second time as if the answer lay there. Suddenly and urgently she wanted more than anything to be on home ground in Poplar.

With a final glance towards the station, she turned her back on it, hurrying towards the tram. The journey home seemed to drag endlessly and it was with an enormous sense of relief that she got off the final bus and saw familiar shops and streets.

The summer wind was stronger here, blowing with a knife edge off the Thames. She went quickly past the Emporium, the tarnished golden balls of the Pledge Office and the pub with the patterned glass windows in Chrisp Street. No market today, and she felt vaguely sorry. The Saturday crowds would have blown away the last cobwebs of disquiet which still clung round her. Thoughts of Luke persisted. Worrying thoughts. This time she could not push them away and found herself wishing passionately that she could step back over the past three uneasy months. Remembering the way he used to be – the real Luke. Moments of gloom when he was shut in on himself were rare. He'd always been active; restless; vital. As if so much was happening inside him, it was impossible to stay still. Quietly absorbed when he was working with the wood he knew so well. She loved to watch his skilful fingers turning scraps of oak and walnut, gleaned from work, into smooth polished articles – the salt box that stood on the kitchen shelf; a spectacle case for the Admiral; a treasured doll for herself. It felt like years since that time. He seemed half dead now. Slouching and morose. His face looking as if he'd forgotten how to smile. And because he was her twin she was bound to him in a special way, and she, too, was changed. It was all wrong because nothing obvious had happened. He was still living at home, going to work, eating, sleeping, doing all the ordinary things. Jack was the one who had gone to France. Yet it wasn't Jack who filled her thoughts.

Coming past the corner shop, she turned into the greyness of Golden Street. She could see the railings in front of the house where she lived, and not much further on, the figure of Luke walking towards her. It was rather early for him to be coming home from work and the unexpectedness of meeting him sharpened up everything she had been thinking, and made her see him fresh and clear. Like a stranger – the thought jumped into her mind, coldly unnerving. The spring had gone out of his step, and instead of looking about him in his habitual quick attentive way, he was staring at the ground, shoulders hunched, hands thrust into his pockets, the fire in him quenched. Trudging along. Frowning.

Frightened and wanting to stir him back into liveliness, she called out to him:

'Luke . . . Luke . . .' and began to run.

2

'LUKE! Wake up ... Luke. Lucas!' Bella shook the shadowy lump in the bed with no more response than a grunt and a muffled:

'Lemealone.'

Outside, the cloudy sky was striped with conical searchlights that crossed and recrossed, transparent as ghosts. In the distance a thunderous crump was followed by another. Now she could hear engine noise clear enough, a rasping chunkety sound that trundled across the night air. Chilling. Fearful.

'It's the Zeppelins, Luke. Wake *up* can't you!' In desperation she tugged at the bedclothes, but he was crafty and had rolled into them, hanging on grimly. 'Oh I know yer awake. Here – I'll pour water on you in a minute.' She made as if to grab the enamel jug from the washstand.

He came up out of his cocoon long enough to say: 'You do and I'll stuff yer head in the po!'

She let go and darted across the bare attic floorboards to the window. Neither of them would carry out their threats, but she knew she was defeated and in any case wanted to see more of what was happening. There was no moon. In place of its light a dull reddish glow had turned the grey roof-slates to amber.

'There's fires over the river, Deptford way. Bomb fires,' she reported. 'Look. *There it is!* Why ain't they firing at it?' She stared at the airship caught in a ray of light. It seemed to hang motionless like a distant silver sausage. Then it was gone, swallowed up by cloud. Another sound now. The rough buzz of an aeroplane, in turn followed by a booming crash which rocked in her ears. She pulled the old dress turned nightdress tightly round her skinny body as if for protection.

'Everyone's coming out in the street. You should see Ma Liggins. Cor she don't half look funny. She's got a bonnet on with a feather over her curling rags, and her nightie's come out of the ark. Bulging out all over she is. Shut yer door y'silly old bag! Somebody'll start calling you a spy before long – letting all that light out!'

'What you need is some net curtains and a pair of opera glasses,' Lucas said and burrowed deeper. 'Shurrup and hop it!'

Plenty of folk are doing the sensible thing, Bella thought, ignoring the instruction. Off to the church crypt, where she and Luke and the Admiral should be going. They were barmy staying here. Sitting ducks. She half turned, meaning to plague him again until he gave in, but the words died. Turning back she flattened her nose against the window, peering obliquely down the street towards the derelict German bakery. She couldn't believe it! Smoke was rising from the chimney. Smoke that was no part of fires caused by bombs. Spiralling smoke that came from a fire properly laid in the kitchen grate. But the place had been empty ever since it was smashed and looted in revenge after the *Lusitania* was sunk. She strained to see more. Nothing. Yard and bakehouse were shadow-black and still. No. There was something ... a small light, a definite dark shape against the cracked glass of the kitchen window.

'Someone's in Friedrich's,' she whispered, unconsciously dramatic.

'Can't be.' Lucas was wide awake and sitting up. In the almost dark she saw him naked as he got out of bed before he wrapped a blanket round his narrow body. He joined her at the window.

'I saw.'

'Yer always seeing fancies.'

'Not this time. There *is* smoke. See for yerself. And don't tell me it's all done with mirrors!' She was cocksure enough to argue, having stirred him out of bed – until another gut-shaking crump sent her butting against him for comfort. He hugged the blanket, his free arm sliding round her. The shivering of her small body ran into his own, rousing exasperating protective feelings. He didn't *want* them. They were a distraction.

Bella could feel the tension in him; knew he was alert and wary as a fox. His mood became her own as it often did, making her heart thud, her breathing quicken. The old frustration hit her. Why couldn't she read his mind as easily as his feelings?

He said abruptly: 'It's probably only kids. Get some clothes on and go and shelter in the church. The old man'll be shouting in a minute.'

'Kids wouldn't...' she began and stopped. Kids would. Kids were game for anything. Hadn't she gone with Jack and Luke down to the wharf with that raft they'd made, for a joyride? Almost drowned too, because the planks were rotten and they hadn't lashed them properly.

'Don't say nothink about the smoke, will you?' He was offhand, but she knew he didn't feel like that inside.

She said: 'If it's kids we oughter do somethink, because of the raid.'

'They'll hop it now. You see. Ain't nothink to worry about.'

'Luke Knight, you know there is. Besides, what if it ain't kids? What if it's a spy?'

'Chrissake, Bella, yer getting like all them gossipy old hens up and down the street. Go and get yer clothes on.'

'And you.' She wasn't going to let him be the only one to do the ordering.

'I ain't coming.'

She felt alarm flare up. 'Why not? You can't stay here. Them Fritzes might come this way. Supposing you was in bed and the house got bombed. You'd be flattened. Killed. Luke, you can't...' Without realizing it, her voice was getting more strident.

He said in a harsh whisper: 'Shurrup! Yer making enough racket to be heard down at the docks.'

'But...'

'Shut it and get!' Anxiety pumped from him into her as he held her tighter than ever and she understood that there was something really wrong; something outside their shared fear of the Zeppelin monsters. She never had these positive convictions about anyone else – only Luke. Because they were twins, she supposed, though it didn't seem to work the other way round. But then he was clam tight when it came to speaking his thoughts.

He let go suddenly, as if realizing he was stopping her from obeying, and gave her a push towards the trap door and the ladder. At the same time the Admiral's voice floated up; a rich gusty Bristol drawl:

'Bella ... are thee up there?'

'Told you!' Lucas gave her another shove.

'I ain't going if...'

'*Go!*' he hissed, this time shoving so hard she was forced to move to prevent herself from falling. Two rungs down the ladder she paused.

'You won't stay up here ... promise?'

He didn't answer and went back to the window, staring out in an agony of impatience which she sensed but couldn't understand. She saw him outlined – thin shoulders slightly hunched; hair a bird's nest of irrepressible frizz; ears cupped as if he were constantly listening.

'Bella me linnet, where's th'clothes? I'm all ready and look at thee! Not even a shawl.' The Admiral was towering towards her, his corpulent figure stretched with shadow drawn by the lighted candle he carried in his only hand. The other sleeve of his shirt dangled loose and empty over the straining waistband of his trousers. His feet were thrust sockless into unlaced boots, and under the shelter of his treasured tricorn hat – a relic from his Grandmother Jess and always worn in moments of trouble – dark cheeks and chins merged into a bull neck. He watched her gain floor level.

'Where's the lad?'

She shook her head, not wanting to say he wasn't coming, and tried to slip past. 'I'll get dressed.'

He wedged the passage with his bulk. 'Is *he* getting dressed?

Them Frenchies'll be here and then he'd best look out if he don't hurry.'

Bella didn't bother to correct him. 'If they do they'll catch me in me nightie at this rate, then there'll be fun!' She tried to ease by again, but he still didn't move.

'Taking his time, ain't he? Can't hear un. What's he up to? If he's messing about with them daft bits o' wood I'll leather him I promise . . . though he is all but eighteen and fighting age. Head in the clouds half his time. If me legs were more trusty I'd be up them rungs . . . LUCAS!'

The final roar made Bella jump. Torn between her desire to protect Luke and nerves that were on the hop, she summoned her cunning.

'You've forgotten half yer bits. Left the Gladstone bag. I'll nip and get it while you see as everythink's all right downstairs. There's a crowd in the street like morning. Ma Liggins is looking like nothink you've ever seen!' To her relief the ruse worked. He stumped towards the stairs which led down to the single room on the ground floor, his heavy tread continuing into the basement kitchen.

When she got there, dressed and carrying the Gladstone bag, he was stirring the embers in the range. 'Might as well have a cupper tea, girl, afore we sets off. Here . . . give us that!' He took the bag, putting it on the table. With the skill of long practice, he flipped it open one handed and ferreted about inside.

'There ain't time, Grandad.'

'Time can be made for what's important. Checking's important. Supposing we got to the church and found summat were missing? Thee see to the kettle, there's a good girl.'

Oh Gawd it was hopeless! He'd never been the same since that dreadful day last summer when she'd got back from seeing Jack off to France and found him at the bottom of the stairs spark out. Concussion and pneumonia to follow. He'd got over those, but something wasn't right. Cracks in his thinking. Shifts in his notion of time. The impossible was happening and it frightened her. For as long as she could remember he'd been like a rock supporting them all, and now he was in need of a prop himself. Luke didn't seem to notice, but then he was shut up in his own head most of the time. She rattled the poker through what was left of the fire in a fury of frustration, killing the last of the glow.

'Grand!' The Admiral had laid out the old leather pouch, the clay pipe, the sovereign in a little bag of plaited hair, and was uncurling the worn creased poster, spreading his vast docker's hand to keep it flat. 'He must've been summat worth watching.'

'You'd never know from that,' Bella said irritably, looking over his arm at the fading wood-cut figures, which were supposed to represent two bare-knuckle fighters, and the uneven grey lettering.

He glanced at her; on the defensive. 'What d'thee expect after more'n a hundred year?'

She was straining after sounds. Bombs. Planes. Gunfire. Luke. The effort shredded her nerves, knowing they ought to be hurrying down the street, not hovering on the edge of old tales he was forever yarning about. She could feel one dangling in the air now and said roughly:

'Dunno why you bother with all that stuff. It's over. Finished. Nothink to do with now.'

'Th've no right to say such things. He was me Grandad like I'm yourn. He made our family didn't he?' The Admiral tapped the darker of the two shapes on the paper with his thick forefinger. 'Slave he might've been, but that don't matter. He were a real man were Midnight. A real man ... and a fighter. He knew as anything worth having has to be fought for. And I'll tellee summat else me girl – things were a sight harder in them days than they be now, but he didn't hang back never, specially when he were out there in the ring. Bare knuckles it were in them days.' He let go of the poster, hooking with knotted fist at the air. 'I tellee it were tough and bloody, but he never flinched. He were one of the best. Clever too – educated he were. A real man all round.'

Poised on the staircase, Lucas could hear the deep voice rumbling out old phrases, and felt an upsurge of the rebellion that had been forming in him for months. The past. Always the past. Rigid; immovable; there like the grey streets, the rain, the war. And always everything boiled down to a punch-up. You fought for your bread, your rights, your family standing ... especially *that*, when your skin wasn't white. The old man expected him to conform – all of them. Jack had, but Bella wasn't wholehearted. He could hear resentment in her voice now as she said:

'Then why did he leave Grandmother Jess, and her up the spout? I don't call that fighting. I calls it running away.'

Anxiety overtook rebellion and Lucas moved with careful steps down to the front door, opening it with breathless caution.

Bella's alert ears caught the quiet closing click. Nipping across to the window which looked out into the area where stone steps led up to the street, she was in time to see Lucas slip like a shade, not towards the church, but in the opposite direction.

Somehow she knew he was going to the bakery, and was eaten up by curiosity and alarm. The Admiral was still fidgeting with the poster. Getting him moving would be like prodding an elephant with a pin, but she couldn't leave him. Chained, that's what she was. A piece of rope between their tug-o'-war!

'Come *on*, before they makes us pancake flat ... please?' the last in a beseeching tone because it was the only way, and because she was feeling slightly ashamed of scoffing in such a mean way at the things he held dear; privately sighing with relief as he tidied up and snapped the clasp of the bag.

When they arrived, the door in the church porch was open. A few people were hurrying through the iron gates and up the flagged path. Coming out to meet them was a faint smell of incense fringed by a stronger smell of mushroom dust, and over the narrow arched doorway in the far wall inside, a single globe of gaslight sent out inadequate rays. Bella knew what she was going to do. She had her hand slotted into the crook of the Admiral's arm, walking with him into the church through the Gothic doorway and down the steps leading to the crypt – no more than a black pit in the gloom.

A man's voice called out: 'Mind where you put yer feet. Shine the lantern up a bit this way, Billy.'

The Admiral took his time, feeling for each step with deliberately over-cautious care. Once in the crypt, light from two more storm lanterns revealed rows of wooden chairs with hymn-book ledges, facing a recess where a pile of coffins was stacked. A red fire bucket had been tucked behind a rough sacking screen for privacy and was already being used. She couldn't see, but she could hear, because the conversation of the crowd – standing, sitting, wandering – was church-hushed.

'*He*llo, Bella, dearie! I wondered if I might come across you and Horace.'

'Auntie Lil!' Bella put her arms round the plumply comfortable bulk which had emerged so unexpectedly from the shadows, and hugged it. 'What you doing round these parts? Thought you was tucked up nice and safe down in Kent.'

'Where's safe these days, tell me that? Besides, I came visiting an old flame. Don't look so surprised, there's life in the old bitch yet ... and mind me hair-do. Took me half an hour that did. Like it?'

Bella stood back and considered the artificially reddened curls, the elaborate veiled hat, the shabby-smart clothes. 'Yer dressed to the nines, Auntie. The middle of the night too – bet you've been out collecting the hearts!'

'Cheeky young devil!' Lily patted her hair. 'Well?'

Bella looked through the flattering veil at the strong once-handsome face, now run to fat and pock-marked with a lifetime of stage make-up. Lily Lucas of the Music Halls, who'd never joined the family feud begun when her sister up and married a darkie who'd had the impudence to give her three kids and die soon after. Good old Auntie Lil, who'd fed Bella jellied eels, stout and theatre gossip, and taught her to high kick like a trouper. Bella smiled broadly.

'Devi, that's how yer look ... just devi!'

'Hark at her, Horace. Right little flapper ain't she! Got all the jargon off pat.' Lily gave one of her rich curdled chuckles that was irresistible and Bella hugged her again because she was glad to see her, and because now it would be easier to carry out her plan.

'Sit thee down, m'dear.' The Admiral was all shining smile and gallantry. He'd always had a soft spot for Lily. 'Tell us about th'self. There's a couple o' seats free. Look after me bag while I fetches another.' He set the Gladstone down, and in the brief seconds he was gone Bella said low and urgent:

'Do us a favour would you, and keep him talking while I nips back home? I know I left the gas burning. If I was to say, he'd carry on somethink awful and want to go back himself. He ain't fit y'know.'

Lily looked at her shrewdly. 'I can see that. He's altered. So've you.'

'Ain't we all,' Bella said, slightly shaken.

'I heard he'd been ill. Met Dolly Burrows down Chrisp Street and she told me. I oughter've come round but yer other Gran . . . well you know how she is.'

Bella did know and didn't want to talk and raise up family bitternesses that should have died along with her Ma years back.

Lily's mood lightened. She gave Bella a nudge. 'If yer going you'd better move sharp, before he's back. We'll have a good long gossip after. Talk over old times. Gerroff with you, gal.'

'Thanks. Shan't be long.' Bella slid behind and away from the Admiral as he came back with a chair hooked over his arm, making for the stairs where, looking back, she caught Lily's eye. A mad ridiculous impulse swivelled her round. Hitching up her damp cotton skirt she kicked once, shoulder high, then bolted up the steps not waiting for any reactions.

Out in the street the night air had a tang of the river as a cool wind blew from the south-east. Gunfire and the crump of bombs had ceased, but the streets were dark and almost totally deserted. Moisture lay on the air. Fine beads of it clung to Bella's hair and clothes as she ran away from the church, past old hoardings advertising Mazawattee Tea and pleas for volunteers.

'To the Young Women of London.
Is your Best Boy wearing Khaki?
If not don't you think he should?
If he does not think you and your country
are worth fighting for, do you think
he is worthy of you?'

Uncaring, unseeing, she sped, slipped, righted herself and sped on again over mud-greasy chaff dropped from the nose-bags of patient daytime horses; over the cobbles and past the corner shop, turning into Golden Street. Her street, whose name she'd always thought a bad joke. Past her darkened home and the Liggins's; past the Irish house and old Ma Burrows's, scudding to a panting halt outside the bakery.

Blind boarded window-eyes and the fire-blackened door-mouth sealed with nailed planks. She knew rather than read the sprawling dirty whitewashed letters across the scarred brickwork – DETH TO KIZER BILL. The place stood silent. Deserted. And yet Luke was there. She was positive. No way in except round the back through Ricker's Alley. A second's hesitation because it was night and Jack's bogeymen, so vividly described and never forgotten, leapt into her mind.

'Daft babbie,' she said under her breath. And went.

In the alley the sagging gate was ajar. She slid through, remembering. Mein Schätzchen monkey, Mr Friedrich had called Luke as he perched on the gatepost accepting knobs of crusty bread hot from the oven. Other less pleasant memories took over. A crowd out of its mind with hate. Mrs Friedrich, blouse torn, hair tumbled, being dragged along the pavement. Glass everywhere. Glass and ugly shouts:

'Kill the Hun ... kick the bloody door in ... bread ... take the bread and put a match to the place ...'

Bella forced herself back into the present, picking her way across the vandalized yard, avoiding the rotting wreckage of old bread trays, sacks, broken flowerpots. The kitchen window was starred with cracks. No light came from behind it; no smoke drifted up from the chimney. But there were voices; one of them Luke's. She crouched under the windowsill.

'Bombs stopped some time back. Listen!'

Lucas listened eyes fixed on the shadow-shape sitting with long thin feet hooked over a rung of the stool on the opposite side of the fireplace. The fire was a heap of damp dead ashes now. The candle safely snuffed. He leaned forward, away from the broken struts of the chair back. 'No planes neither.'

The shadow stirred restlessly. 'You should be getting along. Don't want yer folks back first. You've done more than enough coming to warn me.'

Lucas knew this was right, but the temptation to stay on and find out more ... learn more, was too great. 'It'll do in a minute. Go on about yer job. How long have you been a stone mason?'

'Nigh on twenty year. Apprenticed at fourteen.' The shadow laughed, a low bobbing sound. 'So now you know me age. Dad was set against me being a docker. He'd had a bellyful himself.'

'Grandad's a docker,' Lucas said. 'Or was till the accident.'

'Accident?'

'Box of bananas fell on him when he was down in the hold. Crushed his arm. They had to lop it off.'

'And I bet he's been out of work ever since.'

Lucas said defensively: 'Oh he gets the occasional job. We manages all right, Stan, don't you fret.'

'Occasional job.' There was disgust in Stan's voice. 'What good is that to a bloke in his prime? There ought to be proper provision for accidents ... and a good pension scheme. I tell you, the working man is a fool to himself. Ground under, that's what, and he just can't see that the power's in his own hand.'

'Oh come on, Stan. We've been over all that stuff. Tell me some more about the marble. What did y'call it ... Purleck?'

'Purbeck. I know a red herring when I sees it! I give in this time, but it don't mean I approve of blinkers. You want to take a good clear look around you, mate. Look at yerself, yer wage packet, yer working conditions.'

'Purbeck,' Lucas persisted. 'Nice sound to it. Like using it do you?'

'Single-minded beggar ain't you?' There was amusement in the quiet voice. 'All right ... lovely stuff, but it ain't the permanence of granite in my opinion. Now you tell me somethink. What's got you so all fired interested in stone? Thought you was an apprentice cabinet maker.'

'So I am, but what you've been put to ain't necessarily where yer heart lies.' The darkness was beguiling. An island marooning them both. He'd never told anyone before of his dream that had been born that long-ago day when old Knocker's even older brother had taken him on his barge up the Thames and let him loose for two hours with a twopenny fortune and instructions not to lose himself. He had walked up Millbank and, arriving at Old Palace Yard, was stunned, overwhelmed, by the giant bronze statue of Richard the Lionheart. His whole body had tingled as he walked slowly round, staring up at the ever-changing forms. He felt light, hollow, as though he was about to float into the air. He had leaned against a wall to steady himself, spellbound, thinking of what kind of man could make such a thing. He must have stood there for an hour, eventually walking on up Whitehall to Trafalgar Square feeling strangely different, but in no way afraid.

'You mean you'd rather be a stone mason?'

All the piled-up longing pressed from within, but Lucas still hesitated, finding it hard to actually say the words.

'I want to make statues.' It was out. His treasure. The secret he'd never before admitted, even to Bella. He was afraid now. The dream had been with him so long, but he'd had no way of making it solid. Suppose Stan scoffed; told him he was floundering about in makebelieve stuff, like Bella did in those moving pictures she was forever seeing and going potty over?

'This bloody war,' Stan said with soft venom. 'If it wasn't for that I'd take you on meself. Learn you all I knows about clay, bronze and stone. Put you on the right road.' He got up as if impelled by something outside himself, and knocked over the stool. The clatter exploded on their ears. 'Gawd streuth!' They froze.

'It's all right,' Lucas muttered. 'But I'll make sure.' He stood up meaning to leave, but Stan caught his arm.

'There is somethink. I heard.'

Scarcely a noise. More an undefinable feeling of presence. Lucas jabbed towards the black hole leading into the passage, then indicated he would confront whatever lay outside. As Stan melted into the darkness he moved swiftly, flinging the door open and rushing out so fast that Bella had no chance. He knew it was Bella almost before he clapped eyes on her, and certainly before he grabbed her.

'What the bloody hell? You've no business here.'

'I have, I have ... as much as you!' She was shrill with fright and indignation.

'Keep yer voice down.' He pulled her to him, more to shut her up than to reassure her. 'Here, did you tell the old man where you was going?'

'Think I'm daft?' She pulled away as if he'd insulted her, still trembling. 'Who's that bloke?'

'What bloke?'

'Come off it. Him inside. I saw.'

'None of yer bloody business.'

'It is.' Her voice was rising again and he whispered:

'All *right*. Stan,' tossing the name at her in a way that he hoped would discourage further questions.

She refused to be squashed. 'Stan who?'

'What does it matter. Just Stan.' He was moving towards the gate, pulling her with him.

She stumbled and almost fell, but it didn't stop her questions. 'Why is he hiding there?'

'Oh use yer loaf!'

'I *am* using it.' She resented his scorn. 'What d'yer mean ... that he's a thief? Don't make sense him hiding out there.' She caught his arm, trying to make him stop and face her. 'Tell me!'

He shook her off, turning down the alley. 'Never thought you was that much of a duffer. I said you shouldn't've come, but now y'have, just shut up about it. Understand? Shut up ... or it'll be the worse for us all. Specially *him*!' jerking his head back towards the bakery.

A small trickle of understanding reached her, growing and spreading. 'He's on the run, that's for sure, and if it ain't from somethink he's done, it's somethink he don't want to do.' She grabbed his sleeve, hanging on this time. 'He's a deserter ain't he?' The contempt in her voice was searing.

Lucas halted. 'No he ain't. He's never been in the army because he don't believe in killing. He's a Conscientious Objector if you must know.' He used the phrase carefully because it was important to him to be clear and precise.

It couldn't be true! A conchie ... Luke mixed up with a *conchie*. She realized exactly what he was admitting. He was breaking the law.

'*And you've been helping him!*'

In the darkness Bella's face was no more than a deeper shadow, but he knew without having to see that her full mouth would be pursed tight and the delicate flare of her nostrils pulled down. The disgust and disapproval flowing from her met him like a physical force, but instead of swelling his original anger that had begun over her snooping, it filled him with a hollow sadness. There was no point in telling her any more. He knew there was no way she would ever understand.

In silence they continued along the alley; along the street; pausing for no more than a second at the railings outside their home. Then, in silence, they parted. Bella returning to the church, while Lucas went back to bed.

3

It might never have happened, the way we've slipped back into ordinary life, Bella thought as she bent almost double catching the last of the light by the window. She rethreaded her needle and knotted the end of the cotton. If only she could pretend it was all a dream ... a snatch from what she'd seen last week at the Star Picture Palace. Three days since the Zepp raid. Three days of brooding over what Luke had done. She shivered. How *could* he? Nearly all the men had to join up ... it was the law. His turn was on the way in less than six months. Eighteen on the eighteenth of January, him and her both. Then what?

She sewed over and over to secure the button she was putting on the twenty-fifth shirt of the day. There'd be another twenty-five tomorrow and the day after that ... and the day after that. She fished after the scissors and dropped them. 'Oh bloody Ada!'

'What's got into thee, me linnet? Talking like that! 'Tain't right. Th'bin all wrong side out these past few days.' The Admiral lowered his newspaper, which she knew had been only a barrier between them. It was too dark to see for reading except by the window.

'No reason. The war ... I dunno.' She shrugged, hoping he wouldn't probe.

'We had a letter from our Jack today.'

'I knows.'

'He'm well and no harm come to him.'

'I *knows*.' Aware of the reproach she pushed needle and thimble back in the old cocoa tin along with her sewing bits and got up, going to stir the stew simmering on the range. Luke was late. She stirred rapidly, knowing it couldn't be overtime keeping him. There was less to do at his workshop than any time since he'd started three years back. He was at the bakery. She knew it ... *knew* it!

'What are th'trying to do ... put the fire out?' The Admiral shrugged irritably as drops of stew slopped over the side, sizzling and sending up a smell of burning fat.

Bella knocked the wooden spoon on the side of the iron pan, then put it on the waiting saucer, finally banging the lid back in place.

'I'm fed up if you wants to know. Fed up to me back teeth and further.' She began setting the table loudly, knives and forks jingling, plates crashing about.

'Do th'want to break up the whole house, girl? Go easy, go easy!'

She was at screaming pitch now with him; with the lot of them, Jack included, even though he wasn't at home under her feet. Somehow that was almost worse than if he were. His letter had served to rub in the fact that he had escaped and she hadn't. Grim though it must be sometimes out there in the thick of the fighting, at least he wasn't tied hand and foot to dreary things like washing, cleaning, hunting about for food with nothing in the shops and no money to buy it anyway. As for clothes, she'd reached the stage of darning the darns.

'Dunno about breaking up the house ... the food'll be scorched to a cinder at this rate if Luke don't turn up soon. Why I bothers I dunno. I oughter get a job. I'm a fool not to.' Oh Gawd she sounded a proper nag, worse than old Ma Burrows and she was world champion.

'Nobody's stopping thee.'

Bella's mouth, which was open to say more, stayed open, but the words didn't come.

'See?' The Admiral tapped the paper on his knees sharply several times, then picked it up and pushed it at her. 'Plenty of jobs for women with the men being called up. They'm begging for the likes of thee. Look for th'self.'

She twitched the paper from his outstretched hand, still scratchy underneath her stupefaction.

'CALLING ALL WOMEN,' blared the headlines. 'YOUR SKILL AND LABOUR IS NEEDED URGENTLY IN THE MAKING OF MUNITIONS TO HELP OUR HEROES ON THE BATTLEFIELD. SAVE LIVES BY GIVING TIME. If you can help, sign on at any of the places named below or at any street registration centre . . .'

'Says "the Arsenal".' His voice was still tart.

What had begun as a small family tiff was changed out of all recognition. Her thoughts were reeling about. Woolwich Arsenal was just down the East India Dock Road, not far at all. She could still live at home. But that was crazy. Didn't she crave to get away? She was struggling with this contradiction when her ears caught the sound of footsteps and the click click of the back door opening and closing.

The Admiral was saying: 'I may be knocking on, but I ain't incapable. I've done for meself before and I can again,' in a reproachful voice.

'What's that you've to do?' Lucas asked, sniffing as he came into the kitchen. 'That smells good, Bel. I could eat a horse.'

'Need enough for two, I know,' Bella said.

She saw him stock still and knew the stab had gone home. The small triumph was a shaming one.

He said very controlled: 'Draw the curtains while I lights the gas,' and as he passed her, reaching up to the gas mantle, added quietly: 'Yer wrong there.'

The room brightened.

'Gone?' The word was startled out of her before she could catch it. She saw his frown and the small flick of his head towards the Admiral and knew he was afraid of being overheard. But it was all right. The old man was still preoccupied with her.

'Bella's going to be one o' they munitionettes.'

'That true?'

'Yes.'

'What's fixed yer mind on that?'

She looked at him in fierce despair, feeling his disapproval battering at her. 'Because there's a war on and we should all lend a hand. Besides, I'm sick of being cooped up here.'

'Yes, but that . . . why that in particular?'

'Because they're asking. See?' She shoved the paper at him, annoyed by his stupid questions and upset by her own response which was a mixture of resentment and sadness over the inexorable way they seemed to be drifting further and further apart. Even knowing that Stan, the conchie, had moved on was no consolation. It was quite unbearable. Taking a cloth from the line over the range, she slid out the hot plates from the oven, then began sharing out the stew.

The spur of the moment plan turned out rather differently from the way Bella had imagined. To begin with, it was almost Christmas before she could register as all three of them in turn went down with flu. The Admiral was last and worst. It was a long time before she dared think of leaving him for a whole day on his own. When she did sign on, Woolwich Arsenal had a full quota of workers. So had the chemical works at Silvertown close by. Another thing for which she wasn't prepared was the fact that once registered she must first take a course at a technical school, then go where she was directed, within reason. And reason decreed this aero-engine factory on the outskirts of East London which was a good hour's journey from Poplar and meant getting up at five if she was to light the fire, have breakfast, cut some slabs of bread and marg for midday and catch the right tram and bus in time for the seven-thirty shift. She was thinking of it now, her mind far away, as she ate her sandwiches in the factory canteen during the quarter of an hour midday break.

'Did you see the way he looked at me?' Doris Jenkins asked, leaning across the table and pushing at her already upturned nose. 'As if I'd crawled out from under a stone.'

Bella came out of her thoughts. 'What's that?'

Doris sat back, her plump freckled face touched with exasperation. 'Where were you? Thinking about your date last night? I was talking about old Hedgehog. You know . . . the old fellow with the spiky hair that works the capstan lathe. He's a misogynist if ever I saw one.'

'I didn't have no date. I was home last night. And what's a misothingummy?' Bella asked, mistrusting Doris's glib tongue off which long words rolled with ease. They didn't match up with her frivolous manner.

'Means woman-hater, Bel.'

'Plenty of them here,' said a scrawny little woman with eyes like saucers.

'Oh I dunno.' Bella dabbed at the crumbs she'd dropped on the table with a wetted finger and licked them into her mouth. 'You can't really blame 'em . . . the men in the factory I mean. If we proves to be just as good as they are, then there won't be nothink to prevent them being called up.' She got a small shock of surprise hearing herself speak as if she sympathized with anyone trying to avoid going to the war.

'Well old Hedgehog's got no call to be such a gloom. He must be about a hundred.'

'Perhaps he don't like women doing men's work?' Bella suggested, surprising herself again with her own tolerance. This was only her second day at the factory, but she knew well enough who old Hedgehog was. She had received a few suspicious freezing looks from him already. At the time she had put it down to the colour of her skin, but now she wasn't so sure.

'They probably think we ought to keep ourselves clean and dainty and not meddle with dirty oily machines. We shall get our nice hands all messy!' Doris was scathing.

'That lets me out then,' Bella said. 'Nobody 'ud notice a bit of oil on me. Dead-on match.'

There was a flutter of laughter and a stout motherly-looking woman called Gertie said: 'It's not often one of your sort makes a joke of it. You're a star turn!'

What does she know about it, Bella thought, and wished she hadn't made the joke. She felt rubbed the wrong way and wanted to say something cutting, but was prevented by the buzzer warning them that the dinner break was over.

'Where are we off to this afternoon?' Doris asked, cramming in the last of her sandwich.

'To watch milling for starters,' Bella told her.

'I thought this was an establishment for the production of aircraft, not a bakery.'

'Oh ha ha!' Bella said, and picking up the little cardboard attaché case that carried her food and personal belongings, followed the others out of the canteen.

The shop which contained the milling machine was light and airy. Four other machines being worked by women were housed at one end. The rest of the shop was occupied by men at more machines and benches, and a sprinkling of boys not long out of school.

The instructor, a bossy chinless woman with the distracting habit of blowing imaginary hair from her face every now and again, marshalled the half-dozen newcomers round the milling machine. Bella, tucked at the back, had a view of anonymous overall and cap, and not much else. She moved round.

The instructor said: 'This is Emily Palmer – one of our most experienced women machine operators.' She puffed at her hair. 'Afternoon Miss Palmer. Won't disturb you for long. Perhaps you'd explain what you are doing.'

'Cutting channels parallel to this line here . . . along this piece of steel.'

Immediately Bella remembered the sing-song Brummy voice and the lop-sided smile which came in recognition as the girl looked up and their eyes met. It seemed like only yesterday they had been standing together outside Victoria Station. Bella nodded and said a cautious: 'Hello!'

Emily's smile broadened, but this was not the moment to talk and Bella was relieved. She didn't want the distraction of having to chat when she was supposed to be concentrating on the instructions, neither was she sure she wanted to renew the acquaintance, though she couldn't help warming to the girl. But as the group was about to move on, Emily called out over the machine rumble:

'See yo after.'

Bella was mildly surprised as she always was when people seemed to want her company. Emily was trying to be friendly but she felt a curious awkward reluctance, which faded as they moved away, only to come flooding back when the day was over and, leaving the factory with other workers, she found Emily already at the gate. A soldier was with her – a soldier in the light blue of a wounded hero. She waved and beckoned, effectively squashing Bella's half-born decision to get lost in the crowd.

'Glad I didn't miss yo.' Emily was smiling and shivering. 'Moses! It's freezing out here.' Her breath rose in little ghostly puffs in the clear frosty moonlight. She pulled the collar of her coat more tightly round her throat. 'I don't want to keep yo hanging about in the cold, but I couldn't let yo slip away without explaining why I went off that time without a word. It must've seemed so rude. I don't want yo to think ... to imagine ...' she gave an embarrassed laugh, seeming not to know how to finish her sentence.

Say it, Bella thought, say yer afraid I'd think you didn't like the colour of me face! She felt disappointed and realized that at the back of her mind she had been hoping Emily would prove different. Someone who would accept her without the slightest hint that her skin wasn't white.

Emily caught her hand impulsively between both of her own, disarming her. 'What I mean is I don't want yo to think I was being toffee-nosed because we had that bit of a disagreement. I was just feeling ... oh look, why don't we go somewhere warm for a proper chat instead of freezing out here?'

'There's a pub on the corner,' the soldier chipped in. His voice had the same friendly quality as Emily's – medium deep and sing-song.

Emily gave another little stuttering laugh. 'I should've said . . . this is my brother, Vic.'

'Pleased to meet yo.' Bella's hand was taken in a firm horny grip. 'Yo will come, won't yo?' He seemed genuinely sincere.

She pushed back guilty thoughts of the Admiral, Luke and a dried-up supper, along with her usual caution. Curiosity more than anything made her say: 'Thanks very much,' wondering why either of them should want more than a passing word with her.

They moved with the hurrying crowd of workers away from the gates of the factory along the unlit street. The pub stood back from the road. A tall dingy building in need of a coat of paint like so many others; the interior heavy with mahogany panelling inset with oval mirrors etched with trails of convolvulus. Bella looked across smoke haze to the bar and felt daunted by the crowd and the strangeness of being in such a place. But Emily seemed unperturbed and Vic quite at home, finding them seats at a marble-topped table and fetching drinks.

'I didn't ask if yo likes beer? Never mind, it's grand stuff. Do yo good.' He put the glasses on the table and sat down. In the brighter light she could see he was like Emily and yet unlike. The same broad cheekbones and straight brows. The same warm brown eyes, deepset. But there the likeness ended. His mouth, which was small and might have been tender, fell into taut lines as if he were trying to control the corner muscles from twitching, as they did constantly. The tremor running down into his cleft chin. There was none of Emily's country colour, but then he'd been ill. Only his ears were reddened. He had taken off his cap and his cropped hair stood up like a brush. She watched him take a long drink, afterwards wiping the back of his hand across his mouth. Then afraid of being caught staring, she hastily took a larger gulp of her own beer than she intended, swallowing the wrong way. She coughed helplessly and felt a heavy painful whack on her back, hearing Emily say:

'Vic! Yo'll knock her into next week!'

She spluttered: 'Sorry ...' wiping her streaming eyes, very embarrassed.

Vic fumbled about in first one pocket then the other, finally bringing out a grey-looking handkerchief. 'Here, have this.'

She took it and finished mopping up. The handkerchief smelled strongly of tobacco and faintly of kippers. Not a pleasant mixture, but somehow it wasn't distasteful.

'I was in a bit of a state that day,' Emily said, going back to the original conversation when Bella had recovered. 'Yo knows how it is with good-byes.' She spoke lightly, but Bella was aware of some kind of tension. She wondered about the fate of the Flying Corps officer, but didn't dare ask, and instead copied the light tone.

'You don't have to explain. I was wound up meself – seeing Jack off and them soldiers marching with the pipes playing and everythink. Did you think I was off me rocker, going on about wanting to be on that train to France?'

'Yo wanted to go to *France*!' Vic sounded stupefied, and disconcerted, she reacted with slight truculence.

'I still do. I knows it must be somethink awful out there, but at least it's taking a proper part in the war.'

'But yo're working now, helping make aeroplanes. Ain't that taking a proper part?' Emily asked.

Bella saw Vic begin to say something, then apparently think better of it. The muscles of his face twitched strongly and she felt a flick of concern, wondering what she had said that could produce such trouble in another person. She felt confused and anxious and wanted to leave, but hadn't finished her drink. Also she guessed it would look as if she were throwing their goodwill back in their faces if she got up so soon. She wished fervently she had never come. They were both looking at her, expecting an answer. She said grudgingly:

'Yer right I suppose,' and took another drink, wanting to talk of other things, but not able to think how.

'What have yo been doing this past year?' Emily said, rescuing her from one difficulty and dropping her into another.

'Ain't much to tell. Things stayed the same till I came to the factory.' Which was a thumping lie. Everything had changed, with Luke at the centre, but she wasn't going to breathe a word about *that*!

'How was it yo got sent to this particular factory? Did they give yo any choice? What made yo pick engineering?' Emily was overflowing with questions. She leaned forward across the table.

'Didn't have no choice really. I just registered and got directed here, after training. The Arsenal's near where I lives and I wanted to go there, but it was chock-full when I come to apply. Me Grandad's been bad on and off, so I had to wait till nearly Christmas before signing on.'

'And your brother,' Emily went on, 'is he all right?'

Bella felt a cold flood of apprehension before she realized that of course Emily meant Jack not Luke. But her face had betrayed her, because Emily said quickly:

'I should watch my tongue. I didn't mean to upset yo.'

'You didn't. He's fine. We've just had a letter.' Bella took another sip of beer, on the point of asking about the airman now that the ice was broken, but at the last minute lacked courage and instead rushed into telling the news of how Jack had been made a corporal and how he was hoping for leave soon.

When she finished Vic put down his glass. He seemed to have himself under control again, grinning as he jerked a thumb at Emily. 'Yo wants to watch her – she's a real driver. She'll have everything out of yo at the drop of a hat. It's her Suffragette training. Never give up!'

'What tripe,' Emily was very red. 'Don't listen to him.'

'Having me on are you?' Bella looked from one to the other.

Emily went redder still. 'Not exactly. I was a Suffragette, but it's the way he says it ... oh Vic, yo're a great ninny!'

'Smashed winders, did you?' Bella asked, fascinated.

'No, but ...'

'But she did all right,' Vic intervened. 'A real stout heart. Got knocked about and shoved in jug and force fed.' He seemed immensely proud of her.

'I never knew a Suffragette before,' Bella said, her own problems paling a little in the face of all Emily must have gone through. The news forged a bond. As if trouble experienced had put them on the same side. She wondered if Emily felt the same, and then recalled that Emily knew nothing of Luke – was not even aware of his existence. It seemed extraordinary when she felt branded by having a brother who had helped a conchie. It must read plainly on her face, in her voice, in the way she walked. She glanced at them, the ready fear creeping over her, but Emily was busy dealing with her own embarrassment by blowing her nose in an elaborate way, and Vic was spinning his glass. He winked, catching her eye. The nervousness had spread into his movements and the glass clattered on the table. He set it upright then dug in his pocket, producing a packet of Woodbines.

'Smoke?'

Bella shook her head. 'I don't thanks.'

'Emmie don't neither.'

She was glad to hear that. Plenty of women did nowadays, and in public, but it always set her teeth on edge to see them. She watched him light the cigarette, noticing how his hand shook. He looked up, saw her observing him and almost slammed the matchstick into the glass ashtray. The reaction had a violence about it which made her start, and instead of looking away he stared at her, his gaze disconcertingly intimate. He didn't have to make it so plain that she was different. The unpleasant idea came that perhaps this was the real reason they'd asked her to go with them to the pub. Just to see how she worked – like trying out one of those nigger toys that swallowed pennies. It was an ugly notion and didn't quite convince her, but in an attempt to divert this concentrated attention from herself and put things back to normal, she asked Emily:

'What d'you think of factory life then? If I can learn to work a machine half as good as you I'll be that pleased.'

'It's all right I suppose.' Emily was offhand.

Bella was puzzled. It was as though in speaking she had unwittingly raised a barrier. 'You sound as if you ain't too sure. What's wrong with it?'

Emily shrugged, circling her finger round a wet beer ring. 'It ain't all roses.'

'Bound to be hard.'

'Hard slog never bothered me,' Emily said carefully and hesitated again. 'It's helping to make things to kill people I can't stomach.'

'But you volunteered. Nobody forced you.' Bella was blunt with surprise. It was amazing that Emily, who had seemed so modern and capable, wasn't enjoying this new life helping the war effort. And her brother was a Tommy!

'That's true, but things change.' Emily went on messing with the spilled beer.

'Come on now! Don't get so serious,' Vic said. 'Life's too short.' He raised his empty glass. 'Drink up and I'll get another round.' There was a force in the way he spoke, as if it were important to keep skittering quickly across the surface.

'It is serious. She did *ask*!'

Vic said: 'Oh Emmie!' suggesting this was an old argument.

'It's how I feels.'

'But only since ...' He stopped abruptly.

Emily looked directly at him. There was a set calm in her face and she said in an even voice: 'Since Peter was killed. Yo don't have to be careful any more. It's over a year now.' She turned to Bella. 'Yo remember Peter, my friend the airman at the station?' She drew a wet cross then smeared it out with a sudden fist, her voice husky. 'I'm helping to build those very things that shot him down ... can't yo understand, Vic?'

'They weren't British planes, they were Hun, and he was in a kite-balloon not a plane, so yo can't even make sense out of that! It's a good job for us poor mugs that not everyone sees it your way.' Vic shoved back his chair, making the legs screech over the lino. 'Booze. That's what we needs ... blurs the edges.'

'Not for me.' Bella collected her case and stood up. 'I've been longer than I ought already. Thanks for the beer.'

Vic said with real concern: 'Yo ain't going because we're arguing?'

'No . . . no of course not.'

'Because we get along fine mostly. I just have to sort her out now and again. What else are brothers for?' The rasping joky humorous note was back and Bella saw Emily's swift anxious glance that grew into a smile. Vic went on: 'Don't take notice of me sounding off. Everybody's entitled to stick to their own view. Christ . . . what else are we fighting for?'

It's Luke and me in reverse, Bella thought, and the astonishment stayed with her as she said her good-byes and went into the street where the first soft flakes of snow were beginning to fall, remaining with her all the way home. Only when she reached the whitened area steps was she jolted out of her preoccupation.

Voices. Loud voices. The Admiral and Luke! Through the window she could see them either side the hearthrug. Upright. Unrelenting in the lowered gaslight. Someone else as well. Lily – her broad expanse lapping over the edges of the inadequate kitchen chair. Bella took a deep breath, braced herself and opened the kitchen door.

'Thank Gawd you've come, darlin',' Lily said. 'Now perhaps we'll hear some sense.'

'Sense?' the Admiral roared. 'What sense can she hope to get from a bloody conchie?'

Bella said: '*What?*' tense with alarm.

'Him. That stiff-necked addle-pated yeller brother o' yourn!'

Bella looked at Luke. He was bristling. She could feel his implacable determination that was wrapped in fear, dividing herself.

'What he's trying to tell you,' Luke said, flat and colourless, 'is that I ain't going for a soldier.'

It had been spoken at last – the thing she had dreaded to hear. In the gasping silence she recognized with a little flick of surprise first relief, then the fact that nobody else felt the same way. The room was full of screaming straining tension which must be broken.

'What d'you mean?' She heard her voice speak, but it didn't seem to belong to her.

'Just that. I ain't going.' He was aware of her anguish, but could not respond. There was no place, no energy for anything but holding steady.

The Admiral pushed his thick neck forward. 'How can th'not go if th'bin summoned?'

Lucas shrugged his shoulders.

'Answer me!'

'When the card comes I shan't take no notice.'

'But what will th'do?'

'There's nothink to *do*.' Lucas was faintly surprised. That particular question was almost the last he had expected.

'Th'bist afeared?' The Admiral's eyes opened wide in astonishment. 'Th'can't be afeared, boy ... not thee. All them years I watched thee agrowing and never anything th'wouldn't try. Anything our Jack did, th'd have a go at. Remember that time th'jumped off the privy roof, and not much more than five year old? And old Fider, that bloody great doormat ... sent him packing when he had a nip at our Bella. And what about the time th'shinned up that tree after that scrawny bit of a kitten as got stuck – seemed like right up in the sky th'were, thirty foot if it were an inch, but th'didn't give a damn. Th'can't have changed so much. Fighting's in the blood, defending th'self; looking after thy own. It's what th'bin given, fighting blood. A family heritage all the way down from Midnight.' The Admiral was almost sentimental in his pleading. 'Tough as they come right from a little lad. Th'can't be *afeared*!'

'Of course I am,' Lucas said with a touch of scorn. 'Show me a Tommy that ain't. But that's not the reason.'

'Th'bist a coward ... a *coward*!' The old man lost his temper and made an insult of the words. Goading. Still hoping for denial.

'For Gawd's sake, Horace, yer telling the bleedin' street! Bella, can't you stop them?' Lily was out of her chair, clutching at the Admiral, but he shrugged her off, flinging wide his single arm as if to haul in the backing of the world and looking faintly absurd as he did so; voice ballooning:

'God Almighty ... me own flesh and blood. The blood of Midnight; of us all ... our family. Thee and me may talk different, but we'm the same through and through. We'm English to the bone. Turning traitor on thy own country, that's what th'will be doing if th'keep to this thing and then it's dirt on us all. Understand ... *on us all*! And don't fool th'self that means only us three in this room. Fingers'll point at all the coloured folk hereabouts. When summat bad like this happens we all gets lumped together no matter who we be or what we think. By God, of all things ... thee, a coward ... a shifty backsliding shirker! A ... a ...' he choked over the words and Lucas intervened in the same level voice:

'You never asked me why.'

'Why?' Bella said quickly.

'Because the whole thing is a waste ... from beginning to end – ugly waste. What else?'

'What else?' The Admiral exploded the air with his voice. 'I'll tell thee what else.' He loomed over Lucas, who flinched as if expecting a blow but didn't budge. 'Because, by Satan, I'll not house a flamin' conchie ... no, not at any price!'

Bella closed her eyes, fighting to hold her world together; fighting off her own cowardice and a hysterical desire to laugh. She wanted to run because they were as bad as each other, stubborn and mulish, and she was sick of the whole thing. There was nothing to be done with either of them. In the core of herself she felt Luke's terrible immovable decision. It seemed as if she had split in two, the other half being her own self despising her Luke self for this ridiculous and dreadful choice. The dual sensation ripped her apart and she heard Luke's voice as if from a long way off.

'Don't bother yerself. I ain't staying to get you into trouble!'

His footsteps passed quick and light – a draught as he pulled the door wide.

'Luke.' She opened her eyes, but he had gone unheeding into the passage and then the area. The awful laughter pressing against her ribs vanished. 'Luke . . . Luke . . .'

The powdering of snow covering the area steps was stamped with a chain of footprints which lengthened down the street as she reached the pavement. She could see him running with the familiar easy flow, his black shape trimmed with white by the fast falling snowflakes. Then he reached the corner and was gone.

She stood with one hand on the railings, unaware of cold or the revealing fan of light through the door she had left ajar, or other lights furtively coming and going in neighbouring windows. Alone and desolate, she went on standing until an arm slipped round her shoulders.

'Come back inside, darlin',' Lily said, 'before you catch yer death.'

The words sounded oddly. Bella repeated them to herself: 'Catch yer death.' It seemed as if death had already reached out to try and touch her. 'Stupid,' she said quietly, then shouted down the street: 'STUPID!' and went back into the house, slamming the door.

4

THE piece of mahogany clamped to the bench had a particular fine grain and a depth of colour that was rich and wholly satisfying. Its beauty demanded close attention because nothing less than perfection would be right. Lucas selected his favourite paring chisel from the rack on the wall, and shaved a wafer of wood precisely from the through-dovetail joint he was fashioning. It was a section of a small drawer – part of a trinket box he was making as a birthday present for Bella in the moments he could pinch from work; moments that were becoming more and more frequent. The last order had been completed yesterday; an oak china cabinet with carved cabriole legs finished like animals' paws. A wedding present that was destined never to be given because for three days there had been no bridegroom. The war had seen to that. Now there was nothing for the remaining craftsmen to do, and the dwindling business was propped up by an order for coffins. The cold-cooks had a great need of coffins.

Lucas inspected the joint and tried it for fit, mating the tails and tapping them into position, using a square of wood to prevent the hammer from damaging the surface. It was exact.

'Made a lovely job of that, mate,' old Knocker said, stomping across the workshop floor, his wooden leg tapping out an uneven rhythm. He touched the box with a gnarled appreciative hand. 'Nothink comes near a good bit of meoginy. You can show me all the oak y'like. It don't hold a candle to meoginy. Rosewood and walnut are nice enough in their place, but meoginy ...' he grunted approval which turned to a sigh. 'Can't see when we'll be doing proper work agin. Coffins!' He scratched between the cysts on his naked head, squinting at Lucas from under bald wrinkled eyelids.

'Somebody's got to make them,' Lucas said.

'Daresay, but a jobbing carpenter could knock them cheap sort up in a brace o' shakes. Don't take no *skill*!'

It was true. Lucas gently tapped out the section of drawer and went across to the coke stove where glue was keeping hot and liquid in a double iron pot. He began to apply the glue to the joint with a small brush, knowing that old Knocker was watching every move as if he, Luke Knight, was still a raw novice instead of a craftsman apprentice who'd almost finished his time. Coming back to the bench, he reassembled the drawer, cramping the completed carcase in position to dry.

'Present for yer young lady?' old Knocker asked casually.

'Sister.' Lucas smiled privately at the attempt to draw him out.

A grin and a nod. 'Yer a deep un, me old china!'

It was a game they often played. The old fool was determined to get him to admit to a bit of skirt on the side. Convinced that no young chap could ever exist without keeping company with some girl or other. Let him think what he liked. At least it kept him off the birthday that threatened like an unexploded bomb. Three days. All that was officially left of freedom, and he still had no proper plan, only half-formed ideas more like *Boy's Own* adventures than anything else. A numbing sensation spread along his nerve endings at the thought, and in an effort to defeat it he fixed his attention on the box. There it sat. Positive. Unchanging. *Real!*

The door into the workshop pushed open, blowing aside wood curls, sawdust and Lucas's uneasy thoughts. He saw the guv'nor stoop under the lintel then straighten up, slamming the door behind him. The created draught raised a fine dust which irritated the guv'nor's flared nostrils and made him screw them with a handkerchief, afterwards stuffing it back into his apron pocket with a little punch as if the thing were alive and might rear up if not taught a lesson.

'No point in hanging about, Knocker. Shan't start on the coffins till morning.' Jabez hunched his skeleton shoulders and rubbed large gaunt hands, going over to the stove to warm himself.

Lucas began to tidy his belongings with slow deliberation. There was no rush for him. Since the row with the Admiral he'd been sleeping rough in the workshop on a bed of wood-shavings and sawdust, brewing up over the stove and subsisting on bread, what cheese he could scrounge, and pints of crowdie – a soup of anything and everything stewed in water. The old year had come and gone like that; Bella with it. She'd tried very hard to heal the rift and get him back home. He felt a twist of shame remembering her pleading at the workshop door. But he wouldn't go back to be bludgeoned and insulted by an old josser who reckoned brawn any day against brains. He would *not*. The guv'nor wasn't like that. He reckoned the skill in his hands, the joy in fine wood and patient careful work. Lucas looked across at him brooding over the stove and tried to guess his thoughts, but the narrow back gave no clue.

'Night then, guv'nor,' Knocker said, jamming his cap well over his ears as a defence against January cold. 'Mind yer makes out proper with yer lady love, young un!' and with a wink he went out.

As the last tool slotted into place, Lucas paused, looking through grimy glass to a glory of pink and pearl striping a polished sky. Glowing silhouettes of chimney-pots and rooftops littered the horizon – all caught and held in the window-frame. The beauty of it obliterated everything else, shutting him off from workshop and worries, so that the guv'nor's voice came as a shock.

'I've been wanting a word.'

Lucas watched the cropped head with its fan of white up-standing hairs on the crown, pivot on the stringy neck. The loose jowls, thin and flat, shook with the movement, reminding him vividly of Ma Liggins's old cockerel which lived in a beer barrel at the bottom of her yard. He almost expected to hear a crow and felt faint absurd disappointment at the sound of ordinary words.

'About you having to go for a soldier, lad. You're eighteen come Thursday I know, so it may well happen that you'll not be able to work out the week. I've made up your wages till Friday week. Sort of bonus seeing how things are.'

Lucas stared at the little paper packet being held out to him. The impact of the words shattered the comic image of man-cockerel and brought back the fantastic world that seemed to be unavoidably netting him, do what he would to be free of it. He made no move to take the packet. There was a peculiar horror about being presented with two weeks' wages and kindness. He said gruffly:

'I can't take it.'

'Why ever not? You've a right to it, boy.'

'I ain't.' He didn't want to go over the same ground again because it was impossible to make himself understood. But there was no way out. He must forfeit the guv'nor's goodwill and with it his makeshift home. Harbouring a conchie was a different matter altogether from helping out an apprentice who'd had a bull and cow with his Grandad. He took a careful breath: 'When me card comes I shan't take no notice.'

The expected burst of indignation didn't happen. Instead Jabez regarded him for a long moment with what might have been pity. Lucas fended off the thought. That was something he didn't need either. Human emotions had a way of winding themselves round clear fact and obscuring it. Right now he wanted peace and solitude above everything else to help him decide what must be done.

'So that's it,' Jabez said softly. 'I knew something was really up. Religious reasons?'

'No.'

'What then?'

Lucas shook his head, but the waiting silence went on waiting as a thin icy draught licked round his feet, coiling up his legs and into his very bones. He forced out: 'They ain't got no right. This war ain't of my making. I don't want no part of it.' Spoken aloud it sounded weak and without a grain of the burning conviction that was like a relentless force inside him. One life, that's all he had. Just one, and they expected him to throw it away – expected him to be *proud* to throw it away. All of them. Even Bella.

Jabez whistled thinly through his false teeth. 'Know what you're saying, boy? Really know?'

Slapped down like that what was there to say? Conchies were shit to most folk. They got a rough time accordingly, but so did the Tommies. Nothing to choose between them. The injustice swelled up, threatening to choke him, and he stared furiously out of the window, trying to make himself one with sky and buildings again.

Jabez looked hard at him, his face working in a series of small frowns and twitches as if he was trying out different words and sentences. In the end he seemed to give up, shoving the wages back in his pocket and in a couple of strides reaching Lucas to catch him by the shoulders, shaking him hard.

'Maggot-brained little duffer. What's got into you? Need your head stuffing into a tub of cold water. That'ud cool your brains.' The shaking stopped but not the words. 'You want to think before you go round making statements like that. But I know you – got some addled notion that don't even make sense in that fuzzy head of yours and are too self-willed to listen to reason. Stubborn as a donkey. Always were!'

'That ain't true!' The words were wrung out of Lucas.

'Well what is true then? Blab things like that and your life'll be a misery. They'll take you – surely you know that? There won't be any staying at home. Remember Boffy Johnson?'

Frog-marched down High Street on his flat feet, a burly marshal either side hanging on to his matchstick arms as if he had a hope of breaking free. Rotten tomatoes hitting him – and stones. Vanished now with nobody knowing his whereabouts. He might never have existed. Lucas shivered. And there was Stan, carver of gravestones who'd talked of brothers. Not, it turned out, blood brothers, but the underprivileged workers who, according to him, carried the world on their shoulders. He'd gone as well; scared off by Zeppelins and Bella, taking his knowledge with him. The bitterness of that was hard to bear.

'Listen will you!' Jabez seemed strangely frenzied, as if powerful feelings were threshing about inside the prison of himself. 'You *must* go. Use your common sense, boy. The war can't last forever. You've as good a chance as the rest. If the military take you as a conchie they'll send you to the front line and you won't have no Tommy's rifle to protect yourself. Dead as a doornail you'll be inside a week.'

Dead as a doornail whatever he did; it made no odds. If he had to die – and he'd move mountains not to – he'd do it for the right reason, and to hell with the guv'nor's gab or anyone else's. A small wonder crept in amongst the bitterness. In all this carry on the guv'nor had never once waved a flag for King and Country. He felt the long fingers bite into his shoulder-blades. There was no other way but to meet the piercing stare and doggedly resist, without trying to unhook himself. All this and more was bound to happen again – over and over. Might as well start practising now. An unblinking gaze seemed to be the way to wilt the guv'nor's heat. A frail bud of triumph appeared, though the lecture went on.

'Read the papers, boy. Unplug your ears in the street. You'll soon find out what's in store for you. God save us ...' Jabez searched the rafters for inspiration.

Lucas remained still and stubborn, not giving anything of himself and expecting nothing in return. He waited to be told to take himself off, but the old man turned away, going to lean on the bench as if in need of support.

'Argufying,' he said at last, tiredly: 'You'll get plenty of that the road you're taking. And thrashings. No sense in wasting my breath. You can stay on till Friday, but after that I've no choice but to sack you.' He looked round. A brief direct affectionate communication. 'I'm sorry, boy.' Taking the wage packet from his pocket again, he placed it square on the bench, then without another word or look left the workshop.

The sun was a thin lip resting on slates. Shadow wrapped Lucas in a cold dark cloak as he stood motionless, trying to crawl deep inside himself away from the dos and don'ts, the intruding well-meaning misunderstandings, the other people. Lost in himself he remained like that for ten minutes or more, only coming back into the present because the cold was freezing his marrow. Unaware that there had been listening ears, he set about reviving the fire.

5

LUCAS came out of the dingy little grocer's a few yards from the workshop with a loaf of bread and three sausages. He was pleased with his purchase. The loaf was large and the sausages reasonably healthy. A good stodge for tonight with something left over for tomorrow.

Tomorrow!

The birthday. Then Friday, day of doom, when he would be workless, homeless and probably hunted. The thought brought a clutching sickness to his stomach and a restlessness throughout his body. He turned away from the direction of the workshop and walked the length of the street in an attempt to calm himself, taking more than usual notice of the smudged shadows thrown by the uneven shapes of the buildings. Crevices of deep purplish black where secret alleys sucked back from the pavement. A paler striping of railings hinted at by light escaping from an uncurtained window. Instinctively he looked up into the sky, but the cloud was thick and low. There would be no Zeppelin raid tonight, that was one thing he could count on. The only thing. He felt an increase in the nausea, coupled with a faint astonishment that, faced as he was by a future jam-packed with frightening unknown difficulties, as far as his determination was concerned, they might not have existed. The guv'nor was right. He was maggot-brained. Crackers. Ninepence to the shilling. He was also right! The sort of rightness you felt deep in your bones. It was difficult to bring out tidy reasons in words, but the conviction was absolute.

Little curls of fog were drifting in from the river, hazing the street. A damp cold oozed through his clothes. It was no time for walking. No time for letting his fears get the upper hand.

If he was to succeed he must accept them, look at them straight, then kick them out! No one had caught him yet. He might remain free.

He turned resolutely and began to walk back towards the workshop, going up the steps and pushing open the door which he hadn't bothered to lock – then stopping in his tracks.

Bella was there, sitting in the gloom by the coke stove. She got up, seeing him. 'Hello, Luke.' She sounded hesitant, uncertain of a welcome, which touched and irritated him. He was nervous himself, remembering the last time she had come two weeks back. The memory of that bitter meeting still rankled. He said:

'Hello. Didn't think I'd be seeing you here again,' knowing he sounded surly, but unable to help himself. He set the loaf and sausages on the newspaper spread ready on the bench, lit the waiting candle and went to get the saucepan from the nail on the wall.

'I ... I brought you a couple of baked spuds. Here!' She took her hands out of her coat pockets and held them out to him. 'They've kept me warm as toast.'

Her deliberately casual tone; her concern; the familiar little breathy break in her voice which told him how nervous she was – were all warnings. This was to be a final try to get him to come back home. But it was too late. The birthday was tomorrow. He steeled himself, taking the potatoes, only remotely aware of their pleasant warmth. 'Thanks. You ain't gone short have you?'

She shook her head. In the flickering light her small whippet figure looked strangely childlike and appealing. The feeling undermined his stability and sense of purpose. With tight spirals of hair escaping from the scarf shaped to the rounded forms of her head, emphasizing the smooth curve of cheeks and chin, he thought her not pretty, but something better. She was arresting – that was it. Beautiful.

'You've not had yer supper yet then?'

'No. It'll be a feast now. Bread, sausages, spuds and tea.'

'Glad to know you eats well.'

'It ain't always this good.'

They were circling round, each knowing what must come, each waiting for the first real move. Well it wasn't going to be *him*. He'd made it plain last time where he stood.

She sat down again carefully while he rearranged kettle and saucepan on the top of the stove and began to fry up the sausages. The smell was savoury, the sizzle of fat a comforting homely sound. He wished they could continue like this in companionable silence.

'There was a letter from our Jack today,' she said, crushing his hopes.

'Oh ah! Let's have a read then.'

A pause while she twisted her hands together, studiously avoiding his eyes, finally admitting: 'I didn't bring it.'

He turned the sausages with precision before saying: 'Is that supposed to tempt me home?'

'He seems chirpy enough.' She skirted the question, still playing with her fingers.

'Because if it is,' he went on, ignoring her, 'it ain't going to work. We had all that out last time, remember?'

'Don't fret yerself, I shan't forget that in a hurry.' She sounded as prickly as a disturbed hedgehog and he couldn't stop his mouth twitching. She saw. 'And you needn't grin neither. Luke Knight, sometimes you gets me back up so much I could scream!' She seized the loaf and hurled it at him.

He caught it with a little flourish, still grinning. Action was more manageable than cruel biting words. Besides, he never could help seeing the comic side when she got so steamy.

She rushed at him, half-seriously aiming a cuff at his head, which he dodged, knocking the handle of the saucepan so that it spun dangerously.

'Look out! You'll make me lose me supper in a minute.'

'Oh what's the use!' She sat down again on the stool with a thump, shoulders drooping. 'Luke, why are you doing it? Why d'you have to? I can feel it here,' she pressed her fists over her heart, 'but I can't understand.'

Dramatics, he thought, and sighed. 'Let me get somethink inside me first. I'm starving.'

'I'm sorry. But you knows how it is. It's been eating me up ever since I found you in the bakery with that bloke.' She looked at him now, her eyes wide and glistening. 'I can't bear not to know.'

He speared a sausage on the end of his pocket-knife, picked up one of the spuds and perched himself on the edge of the bench, eating with relish. The companionable silence came back and he was reluctant to destroy it, but she looked so anxious that he gave in.

'I can't believe in this war, Bel. What's it got to do with me or you . . . or any of us? I don't want to get killed for nothink.'

'But it ain't nothink,' she burst out. 'If everyone refused to go, them Fritzes would come over here and own us.'

'And if we win we'll go over to Germany and own them. Don't you see it cuts both ways? There's probably some girl over there talking to her brother right now and both of 'em saying the same things.' He shrugged helplessly. 'It ain't nothink to do with us . . . with me. I've got better things to aim for. Things I ain't going to let them take away from me.'

'What things?'

He looked at his hands, knowing she couldn't possibly understand. 'Things I wants to make.'

'What things?' she repeated, voice now edged with exasperation.

He sighed again. 'Statues.'

The following silence was no longer companionable. He knew she was baffled, and was overcome with a sense of hopelessness.

'Of all things. Of all daft things.' She spoke so quietly it was as if she were talking only to herself, which pushed him into saying fiercely:

'It ain't daft. It ain't half so daft to want to *make* somethink as destroy it. Worse than that . . . destroy just because some crazy halfwit you've never seen and never will see tells you to. I won't do it. Understand? Won't!'

She was angry now. 'All right ... *don't!* But I daresay you ain't never given a thought to the rest of us. Mud sticks you know. We shan't escape. You've heard how folk gossip. Just imagine old Ma Liggins when she gets going, and Dolly Burrows. And we've got to go on living amongst 'em. It's bad enough having to walk round in skins that ain't white. Trying not to notice that everyone thinks yer different from the rest. Trying to make 'em *see* as yer just as much of an East Ender as they are. Sometimes I'd give anythink to escape, but I can't. I often try when I'm at the pictures. That's why I likes going so much. You can be anythink in the world when yer in the Picture Palace. Don't matter what colour you are. But it don't last – I'm here and I have to put up with it. Oh ...' the last came out in a kind of wail, cooling his hot resistance. He had never realized before the depth of her concern about such things, and slipping off the bench he came and gripped her shoulders, giving her a gentle shake.

'Don't take on so. They ain't worth it. Lot of blabbermouths, that's all they are. And it don't matter tuppence if yer green with little pink spots neither. None of that matters. It's sticking to what you thinks right that matters.'

She put her hands over her face so that her words were muffled: 'You sounds just like the Admiral. Sometimes I almost ... *hates* you.'

He stepped back and she took her hands away, her voice rough with feeling:

'I would do an' all ... except yer part of me and I loves you.' She got up and walked quickly to the door, opening it, then pausing. 'You won't change yer mind?'

He shook his head, unable to say a word, seeing her turn and the door close between them.

'Yo looks rather peaky,' Emily said, hanging her coat on a peg in the cramped factory cloakroom and unpinning her hat. 'Night on the tiles?'

‘What me?’ Bella tried to cover up by joking. In a twisted way the guess was too near for comfort. ‘When do I ever go out?’

‘Tonight if yo likes. Vic and me are going to the moving pictures. Like to come?’

The invitation capped the irony because today was her birthday. She didn’t know what to say. Ordinarily she would have been pleased as punch. But now! ‘If I’d known before,’ she began, and paused. How to put it without being caught out? ‘It’s me Grandad, see. He’ll be on his own and he worries so.’

‘Won’t your brother be there?’ Emily asked. ‘He ain’t gone yet has he?’ She knew about the impending call-up. Bella had told her.

‘He’s been doing overtime lately . . . certain to tonight,’ Bella invented, praying Emily wouldn’t probe any further. ‘And I’m feeling a bit off. *You* knows,’ she added to clinch matters.

‘Oh I see. Poor duck, having to stand all day too. I’m lucky it never bothers me, but my sister . . . lays her flat. Yo wants to see Mrs Potter if yo feels really knocked up. They’ve made her Welfare Officer did yo know?’

‘Yes. But I ain’t that bad,’ Bella mumbled, slightly ashamed now she had deliberately misled Emily into thinking it was the wrong time of the month. She busied herself taking her overall out of her case, putting it on and going to look in the spotty square of mirror while she tucked her hair under her cap. A dark-brown face stared back; wide eyes; wide full mouth; unruly frizz pushing out round the rim of the cap. Really it was a riddle how Emily could have guessed she felt so rotten. She certainly didn’t look pale! The memory of the encounter with Luke last night surged into her mind, leaving her weak and turning her feelings topsy-turvy so that now she had an overwhelming desire to tell Emily everything and share the burden of this dreadful threat. There was something about Emily which encouraged confidences. No chance of her scoffing, and the relief would be so great. But the moment was past even as she thought about it. The cloakroom began to fill up, and there was no other chance until they were leaving the factory at the end of the day. Vic hadn't yet arrived and they paused outside the gates.

'Yo get home and put your feet up,' Emily said. 'And don't come in tomorrer if yo feels poorly.'

There were fine permanent creases running upwards from the corners of Emily's eyes. Smile lines. Watching them deepen, Bella found the courage to say:

'I've somethink on me mind. Somethink as needs sorting.'

'What?'

The direct question snuffed Bella's courage and she improvised hastily: 'About the men in the factory. They don't seem to care much for having women there. Seem to resent us. That Billy Chalmers was ever so off with me today.'

'Don't listen to him. He's just a windbag. It's only the die-hards and the ones as don't fancy call-up that carry on. Yo don't want to let it bother yo. There ain't been proper trouble for months. When there was, we got over it. Stuck by each other. It's the only way when there *is* trouble. It's always the only way.'

'Is it? You really thinks so?'

The intensity of Bella's tone startled Emily. She said: 'Yes of course,' putting a hand on her arm. 'What is it?'

Her genuine concern swept away the last obstacle. 'What if someone's in trouble, doing somethink you don't agree with ... someone you loves?'

'Oh ... *love*!' Emily smiled wryly. 'When it comes to love, then that's it. There ain't no choice to my way of thinking. Are yo talking about your brother?'

The shrewd guess was unnerving, but there was no going back. In a quiet, almost furtive voice Bella said: 'He says he won't join the army or anythink else.' She looked down at her feet. 'I'm so ashamed.'

Emily didn't reply, and looking up again, Bella surprised an expression of sadness, which at first was bewildering and then, as she began to put two and two together, made her wonder.

That airman – what was his name? Peter? She must be treading on tender places. The thought made her hot with embarrassment.

Emily said gently: 'Does he belong to the N-CF?'

'What's that?'

'The No-Conscription Fellowship. There's a good many thinks like him. Tell him to get in touch. Sylvia Pankhurst'll help. She lives your way – the Old Ford Road.'

'I've heard of *her*,' Bella said, moved by Emily's concern. 'She's famous down our way. When people talk about her they calls her "Our Sylvia" just as if she was one of the family.' How sharp the air was – her eyes were swimming.

'Can anyone join the meeting?' Vic asked, coming up behind and sliding an arm round Emily's shoulders, nodding in Bella's direction. 'Hello again!'

'Hello and good-bye,' Bella said with difficulty. 'I'm just going. Enjoy yerselves.'

'Yo don't fancy coming?' Vic asked. 'It's Charlie Chaplin. He's always good for a laugh. And there's "Perils of Pauline" ... spine-chilling!'

Bella shook her head with regretful relief. 'I'm expected back. Another time maybe.' Now what in the world had made her come out with that?

'Chance 'ud be a fine thing.' Vic spoke quite jovially, but the words struck Bella with cold force. Chance! What chance was there? He was leaving in two days. She would probably never see him again. Not that it mattered to her personally, but there was a horror in the idea that made her flesh creep. Could it be that Luke was on the right track after all? No ... no, impossible!

Emily was saying: 'See yo then. And don't forget.'

It was all Bella could do to answer in a level voice: 'I won't. Tata!' and to Vic: 'Best of luck!' If her eyes had been swimmy before, they were awash now. She hurried off down the street, halfway home before she was able to think over all that Emily had said, and she had got off the tram before the full implication hit her. Emily's 'Sticking together' meant helping, and that meant going against everything she believed. Well, almost everything. There was the matter of love, and somebody had to give way. She couldn't change Luke's half-baked notions nor her attitude to them, but she could stick by him because if she didn't he would be on his own. And that would be more than she could bear. She'd half a mind to go to the workshop and tell him now ... quickly, while she was in the mood and had the chance.

But the chance was gone with a shrill voice calling:

'Cooee ... Bella!'

Bella swivelled round and saw a thin figure in the new shorter skirts, red hair coiled into earphones. She groaned to herself. Of all the luck – Ethel Turner, who'd been such a pest all through the elementary with her weak jokes and nonstop chatter. Nosy too; her beady eyes didn't miss a trick. The last person in the world she wanted to see just now.

'I saw you on the tram,' Ethel said, smiling her eager gappy grin. 'But there was too much of a crush to reach you. I'll walk round your way. Ain't much longer than going straight home.'

Bella racked her brains searching for a reasonable excuse to get away, but there was nothing, and repressing a sigh she began to walk homewards.

6

THE birthday had come and gone, so had most of Friday, and Lucas quickly slipped away from the workshop, avoiding sticky good-byes. He tramped along head down, coat collar turned up, one hand thrust into his pocket, the other clutching the bundle of his few belongings, breathing in great gulps of sharp air as he tried to throw off the tense atmosphere of the workshop which clung like wet cobwebs. He'd felt like a ghost all day – old Knocker refusing to speak, refusing even to look at him; the guv'nor with a face long enough for a funeral. And coffins!

A tin can lying on the kerb was a temptation. He kicked it viciously and saw it spin across the road, seeming to take the old life with it – he wasn't sure how he felt about that. Neither was he sure about where his life was going, though he'd thought till his brains ached. For the next half hour he was going back home to give Bella her late birthday present. The hard shape in its wrapping of newspaper pressed between his arm and ribs. It wasn't a perfect job, which rankled, but there hadn't been enough time for developing a good sheen on the wood. He'd finish it one day – if he survived.

A horse and cart swished by, sending up a fine spray of slush. Lucas drew away from the kerb, threading between a few late shoppers and homecoming work people, his mind on Bella. The division between them was widening all the time. Savagely he wanted to wrench it together; put back the clock; chop away the war years that had changed everything and interfered. Impossible in half an hour, even if luck was with him and he found her alone. He hoped fervently that the Admiral would have gone to the pub. Deliberately he kept his eyes looking at the pavement. Seeing boots, buttoned and laced, skirts mud-edged, a very few trouser legs splashed and grimy, tram-line cracks in the pavement. Not wanting to be noticed by anyone he knew.

The ruse didn't work.

'Hello, Luke! Haven't seen you since Gawd knows when.'

He knew the breathy voice without having to look and swore to himself, saying aloud: 'Whatcher, Ethel,' very reluctantly slowing his brisk pace as she couldn't keep up; tottering on ridiculous high-heeled shoes. She had been a pain in school and, as far as he was concerned, hadn't improved with the years.

Coming close, she leaned towards him, nose twitching like an inquisitive rabbit. 'Where you been all this time?'

'Around.' He wasn't going to stop.

'Thought you'd be in the army by now. Had yer call-up yet?'

He could say 'No,' with honesty, though the card would most likely be waiting on the mantelshelf behind the clock.

'Saw yer Bella yesterday. She seemed in a bit of a groan. All steamed up about somethink. She wouldn't say what. Know what's the matter with her?'

He shrugged. 'She's always up in the air one minute and scuffling in the dust the next.' He wasn't going to say one word about the other night.

Ethel looked at him sidelong. 'Heard somethink about you an' all, down at the baths. Heard you'd got yer call-up and wouldn't go. Is it true yer a conchie?'

'At the *baths*? Who said?'

'Millie Hayes.'

'That blabbermouth! She'd tell a pack of lies about her old woman if she thought it 'ud cause a stir. I suppose she got it from the dustman or round at the corner shop!' He hoped he sounded scathing enough.

'No. From her auntie.'

'Auntie' was old Mrs Burrows from two doors down. She and Dolly, that long-nosed daughter of hers, were the worst gossips in the street. Blimey, he could see them all queuing up for their weekly Friday scrub at the Public, ooing and ahing as they passed this juicy bit of scandal from one to another. And who the hell had told them in the first place? Nobody at home. It was considered a terrible disgrace. Not that who told mattered. It was enough that it had leaked out. Everyone would know soon if they didn't already.

They were coming up to Ethel's house.

'Cheerio then,' he said hastily, afraid that her ma would be on the doorstep before he could get away. 'Don't believe every-think you hears,' speeding up and rounding the corner, leaving Ethel staring.

Strange to walk down Golden Street where he'd lived all his life. It felt as if he'd been away for months instead of a few weeks. He wondered how long it would be before he came again, and then remembered he didn't even know where he was going. The gaslamp near the gate wasn't burning and in the strange luminous light trapped by thickening cloud the line of railings was an eerie reminder of prison bars. Quickly he went down into the area, opened the back door, and going through to the kitchen found it in half-light. A candle standing on the table in the old green holder trailed a thin black line of tallow smoke in the draught. Sitting close to it, sewing, was a plump auburn woman. For a second he had the odd feeling of being in the wrong house. Then he recongized her and, as she looked round startled, said:

'It's only me, Lil. Where's our Bella?'

'Stars above you give me a fright. I never thought to be seeing you back here in a long time. How are you managing? D'you feed yerself proper? Bella don't say much. Like a cupper tea?'

'Don't bother.' The stream of concern was irritating, though he knew she meant well. He set down his bundle, repeating the question:

'Where's our Bella?'

'Not back from work yet.'

'She's late then?'

Lily peered up at the clock. 'Can't see the time. She don't get back all that early. It's a good deal further on than Woolwich. Pity she couldn't have got work there. Nice and handy.'

'Why ain't the gas lit?' He went to the gas-mantel and removed the frosted glass bowl, turning the tap and lighting the gas with the candle. It burned high and as he adjusted the flame it occurred to him that for Lily to be here sewing at this time was strange. He put back the bowl and saw her glance nervously towards the scullery door – another thing out of key. Not like Lily to be jumpy.

She pushed the bit of sewing on to the table and patted her hair – a habit he remembered from long ago. She *was* nervous!

'P'raps I oughter tell you,' she began, smoothing the back of her neck with a plump hand, 'I've come to stay a bit. Horace ... yer Grandad offered when there was a spot of bother at me lodgings today. Ever so nice he was ... offering ...' She ended mid-sentence, but he didn't notice. The impact lost because he had seen the postcard sitting just where he thought it would be, behind the clock. With leaden arms he took it. Name and address on the front. Instructions on the back. Report ... without fail ... barracks ... 20th January ... The print blurred in an odd way, cramping into narrow checkered black worms. He looked away and blinked hard, focusing on the Admiral's bulk coming through the scullery doorway. They stared at each other, equally startled; equally wary.

Lily said: 'He came looking for Bella, Horace.'

'Then he's unlucky.' The Admiral lumbered towards the fire, adjusting his braces and running a finger round the collar-less neck of his shirt. Fidgeting.

The realization came to Lucas that the old man was as ill at ease as he was. He expected another bristling attack and primed himself to remain cool, but instead was confronted with a ground-cutting silence. He saw the old man eyeing him warily and stared back. They were sniffing each other's mood like a couple of mongrels.

Lily had picked up her sewing and taken a few stitches as if to protect herself from the winding tension, but put it down again almost straight away. 'I'll make a cupper tea. Pass the time till Bella gets here.' She got up heavily with a pleading glance at the Admiral, who cleared his throat, nodding towards the postcard Lucas had replaced behind the clock.

'What are th'going to do about it?'

The decision which he'd battered at and walked round for so long was suddenly inescapable. The clear coldness of ice filled him. 'I won't go. If they wants me that bad they'll have to catch me first.' As he said it he knew that all along he'd meant to hide. It was a wild unplanned scheme. Barmy. No more reality in it than one of Bella's Picture Palace adventures. But he'd do it. Anything was better than hanging about waiting.

'Where'll th'head for?'

'Dunno, do I!'

'Then th'd best think pretty quick. They want men that bad, they'd take a wall-eyed beggar with flat feet, never mind thee. They won't let the grass grow. Th'won't be safe on the streets. Get down to brass tacks, lad. 'Tain't no good dreaming. Six bleak months I had on the road when I was naught but a lad like thee. Winter's a bloody cold companion.'

The old man seemed sharper than of late and his concern touched Lucas with astonishment. No lambasting this time. He felt a stirring of the old affection that had been lost under rebellious irritation in the past months. He looked across at his grandfather sitting now in his rocking chair, seeing him afresh. An old grizzled Negro, his armless sleeve tucked into the top of shabby trousers that strained across a pot belly, massive shoulders bowed. The physical strength and gusto that had bullied and supported them all for as long as he could remember had collapsed. Age? Or was it this hammer blow he had dealt at patriotism and strong-arm stuff? He felt disturbed, not wanting to make anyone unhappy. Blood ties . . . love ties – they were the very devil.

'If you needs a bit of help anytime, I'll do what I can,' Lily said, uncharacteristically timid. She seemed all nerves, darting little glances first at him, then at the Admiral, an anxious smile glued on the rolls of her face.

Again Lucas was astonished, both by her manner and offer,

hardly knowing how to respond. He knew he oughtn't to refuse any help, but to accept would be a weakness. The comic side didn't escape him. Lily had spoken out in the old man's hearing without being blasted from here to next Friday! He smiled to himself and mumbled: 'Thanks!' avoiding her eyes and going to sit on the stool beside the range. Might as well be warm and comfortable if he had to wait. He leaned over and pulled his bundle closer, taking out the box in its wrapping of newspaper and putting it on the floor beside the stool, catching a glimpse of Lily's ankles bulging over the sides of her shoes. Another sign of age. Queer to think that it was an experience he would probably never have.

The kettle was steaming and Lily filled the teapot, let it brew, then filled the mugs. She handed one to Lucas. 'There ain't no sugar. You'll have to use yer imagination instead.'

He took it with a grin, seeing her face pudgy and white, then aglow with a scarlet light that bathed the whole room for a breath of time, as if a harvest sun had reared up in the street. A thunderous roar shattered window glass and gas bowl – the gas itself blowing out and hissing. Lily shrieked and the Admiral swore as he got up and stumbled. The noise sank away and there was a hundred-year-long second's silence before other noises came to take its place – shouts, running feet, doors banging, the cries of children, dogs barking.

'Sit still while I turns off the gas,' Lucas commanded. He felt his way across the room, afterwards searching for Lucifers and candle. Meeting Lily's damp shaking hand. He squeezed it to reassure her and himself, then found the matches and struck one. The candle flame swayed and guttered. The Admiral was hanging on to the mantelshelf, a strange grin plastered on his face as if the blast had blown up his wits. But when Lucas said:

'Stay with her while I finds out what's happened,' he came out of his trance with a burst of action and a shout of:

'No!' His massive hand grabbed Lucas's shoulder, trying to press him down. 'Under the table. All on us. Till them bloody Frenchies have gone over.'

Lucas shook him off, noticing the old man's slip then getting it straight away as he ran to the door and the area steps.

Over the rooftops an orange glare was lighting the street enough to see people dazed and terrified, some talking in huddles, others scattering in every direction, making for school, church, anywhere supposed to be safe from Zeppelin attack. Under the gaslamp the cobbles were treacherous with shivered glass and he slipped, bumping into Ma Liggins who clutched him.

'Did you see 'em? Where are they? Can you hear 'em?' hysterically wriggling his arm as if to shake out answers; the curling rags in her hair bouncing about.

'No I was indoors. Dunno nothink. I come out to see.'

'Hiding . . . whatcher bet! Leave him Letty. We don't want no dealings with his sort.' The thin shape and pinched face of Dad Liggins was there pulling her away.

'Whatcher on about?'

'Him.' A jerk of the head. 'Don't tell me you ain't heard?'

'About him being a conchie? Gerron with you! He's here ain't he? Known him since he were a little lad. So've you.' Hands on massive hips, she turned on him. 'Didn't I tell you not to eat them winkles? They always gives you an acid belly and a wicked tongue.'

Dampened, but not finally quenched, Dad Liggins growled: 'Call yerself an Englishman . . . bloody nigger!' He spat on the ground.

Lucas ran without another word, a tiny part of him alerted by this first public threat, but much more alarmed by his fears for Bella. He scanned the sky for Zepps, planes, anything that would tell him if more bombs were to fall; trying all the while to work out the direction of the hit. The glow was south-east – a kaleidoscope of changing colour over the docks. Woolwich way. The way Bella would be returning. He began to run faster as understanding brought a prickle to his skin. The blast had torn down a hoarding and strips of old posters were winding round a lamp-post; yellowish in the artificial twilight. Windows all about were cracked and gaping, curtains blowing forlornly into the night breeze that carried a stench of burning rubber. As he reached the second corner that would take him to the East India Dock road, a driverless horse pulling a totter's cart came careering to meet him, wheels crossing the pavement. He dodged, not bothering to try and stop it.

He looked again, but there was no silver cigar-shape up in the sky, no chunking grinding echo of a Zeppelin engine, or the deeper roar of a Gotha plane. Only the distant clang of fire-engine bells and the growing acrid stink. Lucas hunted through the gaggle of people crowding in through the open doors of the school. He hesitated. It was crazy running about like a demented mouse. If she was all right, she'd turn up. If not . . . A clutching feeling took hold of his stomach, the sensation spreading down between his legs. He was on the point of turning back when he saw her coming past the corner shop. Relief came out like anger and he rushed across to her.

'Where the bloody hell've you been?'

She looked at him as if he were a ghost and said: 'Luke?' in a wondering voice.

'I've been looking all over. I thought you might . . . oh Gawd I dunno what I thought.' He knew he still sounded angry, but couldn't help it. Relief was making him shake.

'Don't go on at me, Luke. I'd just got off the tram when it happened. Knocked me flat. There was a woman with her face cut to blazes with the flying glass, oh . . .' she began to snivel. A thin hopeless sound, the tears trickling down her cheeks, hands at her sides like a little child.

Lucas held her by the shoulders, giving her a small affectionate shake, saying awkwardly: 'I'm sorry. I shouldn't've been so sharp. Don't take no notice.' He pecked her forehead and saw the quick surprised upward flick of her eyelids, then felt her cheek rub wetly against his own.

People were still going into the school. Some glanced in their direction, idly curious.

'We'd best get under cover,' he said, faintly embarrassed b- not wanting to start her off again by pulling away. 'There's the school, though Gawd knows why that place is safer than any other.'

'It's all that wire netting over the rooftop playground. The bombs'll bounce off, that's what they reckon.' She sniffed then rubbed the damp from her cheeks, smiling at him tremulously.

Inside the school an extra smell added to the charred stench drifting in from outside. The old familiar stink of chalk dust, years of unwashed kids and damp lavatories. They went into the school hall and a hum of voices. A man with a hook on a long pole was pushing in and out of the groups of people sitting on benches, kneeling by unrolled mattresses. It looked as if most were preparing to make a night of it.

'Mind yer backs, ladies and gents!' The man with the pole was coaxing curtain rings along difficult rods at the top of high windows.

'There's a couple of chairs spare.' Lucas pointed across the hall.

'If there is they ain't for you. Don't want no conchies here. Go and join yer Jerry friends.'

A grey stubbly jaw was thrust in Lucas's face. He said: 'Watch yer tongue, mate,' to Dad Liggins.

'Don't give me no bloody lip.' Dad Liggins came very close, full of courage because his wife was at the far end of the hall. 'Go and lose yerself. We don't want your sort here.'

A group of interested faces turned to see what was going on. The expressions varied from instant hostility to mild amazement. Lucas saw old Knocker. For an instant their eyes met – old Knocker's guarded and reluctant. Lucas felt hurt, and then slightly shocked that he should react like this. What a fool to let such a thing bother him.

'Who says he's a conchie?' A soldier had come from the back, pushing through the knot of people. He was in shirtsleeves but still wore his cap which lodged on jug-handle ears.

'Know him, don't I!' Dad Liggins said. 'Lives just across

from our house. He got his call-up all right. I knows the woman as brings the post. She told me.'

'Yer a rotten gossip,' Bella said angrily, moving in front of Lucas. 'What business is it of yours?'

She was fluffing up like a fiery sparrow and Lucas wanted to laugh like he always did when she got shirty.

But Dad Liggins was not amused. He was livid. 'Jumped-up little whipper-snapper! You should be ashamed . . . like he oughter when there's decent folk giving their lives.'

'Sodding shirker is he?' The soldier squinted at Lucas as if sizing him up. 'Needs treatment.'

'Shut yer mouth!' Bella said.

The soldier laughed. 'Hiding behind a bit of skirt! That's about yer mark ain't it?'

'He ain't . . . he wouldn't . . .'

'He is y'know.'

'Bel, there's no point,' Lucas said, trying to ease away and take her with him, but the press of bodies was too compact now, and the soldier followed up his advantage by giving him a push.

'Sodding shirker.'

Someone behind said: 'Leave him alone. He ain't done nothink.'

'That's just what we're on about, missus,' the soldier said, grinning at his own joke. Laughter backed him up and he tried pushing Lucas again.

'That's it, Tommy. You show him. Our Charlie was killed out there at Wipers. Died for his country he did, and there's buggers like him too scared to fight like a man. You show him!' A screechy woman's voice.

The soldier clamped on to Lucas's shoulders. 'Come on chum. Out! In here's for decent folk.'

Lucas felt alarm stir in his muscles. He saw Bella claw at the soldier's shirtsleeve, only to be flicked off with a jerk of the elbow like a troublesome fly. Concern for her made him try to wrench free, but other hands were shoving him in the back. Someone gripped the neck of his jacket.

‘Gerrout . . . dirty shirker . . . lost yer balls? . . .’ The catcalls followed his progress over the worn knotted floor as he was crushed and pushed and tugged towards the door. In the background he could hear Bella raucous and shouting:

‘Let him alone y’thickheads . . . let him alone!’

and just before he was pitched into the street: ‘It’s a shame!’ Who had dared to say that, he didn’t know and wasn’t able to find out. Persecution had followed him on to the pavement. He couldn’t make a dash for it, because Dad Liggins was there, and another burly bloke with a toper’s veined nose and bow legs, and a couple of old harridans whose faces he knew, but not their names. They hung about him like leeches, cuffing and swearing. In his efforts to get rid of them he twisted and found himself again face to face with the grinning soldier.

‘See what happens to you sniffin’ conchie sods! Have a taste of this!’ A great fist swung; fingers bunched.

Lucas saw the glint of metal and he ducked, and heard a yell of pain as the knuckle-duster crunched into flesh. He didn’t stop to see who’d copped it. In the momentary confusion he tore from the loosened hands and scarpered through street after street after street after . . .

7

STREET after street. The glow in the sky intensified, changed colour, was hedged by swirling clouds of smoke, the air filled with minute sooty smuts. Without deciding, Lucas found himself impelled towards the inferno. Everywhere there were people – confused, crying, gabbling, busy with broken windows, sobbing children, demented dogs. Street after street. The wreckage and stink worsening. Rafters gaped at the sky, chimney-pots and slates crunched under the wheels of passing ambulances, fire-engines, lorries full of soldiers and police, bicycles, boots. Street after street. Whole buildings now cracked and crumbling, rubble spewed across pavements and roads, blocking the way. He saw a tangle of giant metal worms crazily hanging from an open factory floor; a fireplace obscene and naked against pink wall-paper ribbons; a dented kettle caught on a spar of wood; a twisted pram upside down on the roof of a privy. People digging in the ruins, digging for their bits and pieces, digging for people.

'Hey up, mate. Where d'you think yer going? Road's closed. Can't you see that warehouse ain't safe?' A large policeman blocked his way, pointing down a street in the direction of the river.

'What got hit?' Lucas asked. His own danger faded into insignificance.

'It weren't bombs, it were the chemical works at Silvertown went up.'

'Christ Almighty! How?'

'Only *He* knows!' the policeman said irreverently. 'Now either help or buzz off.'

Lucas moved, slipping down an alley between a split corrugated-iron fence and catwalking a broken wall. At the end was a nightmare landscape, a burning wasteland where nothing remained untouched. Through a hole between gaping walls he saw shattered warehouses, isolated chimneys, a glimpse of brackish water, toppled cranes. Nearer, a bucket and chain gang was working at the end of the wrecked street, scooping water that gushed from a broken main. Fire glowed, billowing flames and smoke, lighting a pub from within, spitting out sparks and hot slivers of glass. Nearer still, a terrace of houses leaned together in a drunken pyramid wreathed round by heaps of brick and wood. A small group of people were burrowing there. An old man with a mac over his nightshirt seemed to be in charge, two women helping him. Another younger woman was nursing a baby under her shawl, crouched by a bit of tarpaulin that had been made into a rough shelter.

Lucas joined the old man, giving him a hand with a large lump of mortared brick, and was accepted with a grateful nod. He could hear small muffled cries from somewhere under his feet and worked energetically, sick at the thought of the child below.

'Cellar,' the old man grunted. 'That's what I'm after. The kid and her ma are down there. Not much further.'

They worked on. Finding first a leg, then a separate mutilated arm and hand, then the whole body of a woman. Together they moved it as quickly as they could.

'Bloody 'ell . . . that poor kid. Her ma must've come up to the kitchen for summat. Left her down there . . . left her for good an' all now.' The old man was shaking his head and one of the women burst into noisy sobs. Lucas's body started to tremble violently and he began feverishly digging again, trying to focus all of his concentration on the trapped child. At last a hole was beginning to appear; a hole that wasn't constantly refilling with debris. He put a restraining hand on the old man's arm.

'Reckon I could just about squeeze through there.'

'You'd never! Ain't enough room.'

'There is if I strips off. Better than digging. That beam's holding steady now, but it won't if we takes any more rubble out.'

They looked at one another. A long understanding exchange.

'Go on then. Gimme yer clothes.'

Lucas's jacket was already flung carelessly down on the rubble. Now he took off waistcoat, shirt and vest, handing them to the old man. 'Got any sort of light?'

'There's a storm lantern. The girl has it.'

'I could do with a bit of light.'

While the old man fetched the lantern, Lucas peered down the hole. It was inky and impenetrable. Uninviting. He shifted, allowing the eerie outer firelight to edge in. Not one beam but two. The other wedged at a crazy angle. Just visible beyond the beams was a pile of laths held together by a skin of cracked plaster. With a bit of luck he would squeeze past that. The light brightened as the old man came closer, asking:

'Where d'you want it?'

'If you could just hold it half a mo, while I gets in.' The awful sobbing had died to a hiccuping whimper, which was more bearable. 'What's her name?'

'Annie. She's only eight, an' all, poor little shaver. Don't tell her that her ma's . . .' he flicked a glance at the gruesome lump made decent now under an old torn mac.

'What d'you take me for?' Lucas began to inch through the small aperture. It was a tight squeeze and a painful one as jagged wood and brick scraped and scratched his body. Hips, then legs. Now it was easier. Gawd it was dark! He'd always hated not being able to *see*. 'Shine it up a bit, mate!'

A sliver of light cut the gloom and he saw that several joists had collapsed, two crossing in an X-shape which supported a mound of brick and plaster and the splintered remains of what might have been a table. Moth-like, his hands felt about and he learned there was enough of a gap to ball up and swivel round. Then he could take in the lantern.

That was better. But what a stink! Sewerage and something

else. Gas! In spite of the bitter cold on his bare flesh, Lucas sweated. If he didn't want to be blown sky high along with the kid, he'd better hurry. He called:

'Annie?' His voice sounded hollow as if he was shouting into a tomb.

A shivering whimper and then a child's voice screeched: 'I wanna get out . . . I wanna get out . . .'

'All right, darlin'. In a jiffy. Give us another shout so I knows which way to come.'

No answer to that but the whimpering went on, so he knew she was somewhere to the right below that heap of rubble. Christ what a lot! Get started and talk . . . talk about anything!

'You got a bobber and kibs, Annie?'

Silence, then a whimpering 'Yes'.

'Me too. Conkers an' all.' Careful, careful. Don't hurry or the lot would be down. 'D'you play conkers?'

No answer.

'I used to have this great monster conker. Real King it was. Licked everyone else's. Hard as nails. Used to split 'em right down the middle. I called him . . .' there was a sudden avalanche of plaster dust and Lucas broke off, coughing.

From outside the old man's voice called anxiously: 'You all right?'

Rubbing his eyes, Luke coughed out: 'Yes,' then when he could see again, moved the lantern. Christ the stink! A door had been twisted from its hinges and lay at an angle, one corner poking through a mass of rubble. He scrabbled underneath and to his relief found a gap. Minute, but a real gap. He scrabbled some more. Steps!

'You still there, Annie?'

'Yes. What did you call yer conker?' The voice was much closer.

'King Iron. Good name, eh? He was like iron.' A real hole. But careful or the whole flaming lot would come hurtling down. There was enough up above to bury them both ten times over. He moved the lantern again, peering into the gap, and glimpsed a wraith-like face. 'Hang on, darlin'. Can you wriggle through here?'

'Can't reach.' She began to wail: 'Can't . . . can't . . .'

He realized that the rubble must be well above floor level. There was nothing for it, he'd have to try and lift her somehow. He lay on his stomach and pushed an arm through the gap. 'Come on. It's time to climb the mountain. Grip me wrist really tight.' Small cold fingers found his arm. 'That's it. Now when I say, try and get yer foot up a bit while I pull. Ready?'

'Y–yes.'

'Heave!' He had taken the precaution of tucking his feet behind one of the joists, praying it wouldn't give. It didn't, but as the weight on his arm increased, straining through his body, there was an ominous creak.

It seemed like a year before her head appeared and she was hanging over a hillock of unseen rubble at the back of the door. Dust was starting to fall again. Gawd let it hold! Shoulders now. 'Be a snake ... wriggle with me.' He was backing cautiously.

From overhead a chunk of lath and plaster broke, fell and narrowly missed his head. Annie gave a little gasping cry. He began to curl up in the first small cave, still pulling – but more gently because she was helping herself – until she was free of the door and was pushed up against him. It began to rain plaster in small hard lumps. A slithering overhead was a warning that they were on borrowed time. It was difficult to move in the confined space, but he managed to half hotch, half roll with Annie clinging to him like a little monkey. She didn't want to let go and was whimpering again, but he forced her round towards the last small tunnel, unpinning her arms.

'Go on. Through there.'

'I don't wanna . . .'

'Go *on*!' He gave her a shove and heard her cry out, but saw with relief that she was crawling easily enough. The plaster rain became hailstones and then a waterfall. Something heavy hit his leg with an agonizing numbing pain, but he managed to inch after the skinny legs and saw hands grasp and drag her through the opening. Air met him. Blessed air that was only fresh by contrast. A couple of feet and he would be in it. He thought – Chrissake the lantern! But there was no time and no means of rescuing it. A roar and clatter of collapsing masonry spurred him on and at last he was free. With a final spurt of his flagging energy he shouted: 'Gas!' Staggering to his feet and away, slumping down behind a hill of rubble, hopefully out of the danger zone.

When he recovered enough to look round, the women and Annie had disappeared, but the old man was crouching beside him. The roar and crackle of fires could be heard all round, but the explosion he had expected didn't come.

'Thanks, mate,' the old man muttered in his ear, his breath harsh in his chest. He stared at the place where his home had been, shaking his head. 'Yer a bloody hero!'

'Anybody 'ud've done the same.' Lucas wished he could have slipped into the darkness. He didn't want gratitude.

Neither of them spoke again for several minutes. The old man only gradually digesting what Lucas had said. 'Them's just words, mate. You *did* it,' he said at last. 'Kaiser Bill'll have to look out when you joins up – won't know what's hit him!' He began to cough – a hard bubbling sound.

'You wants to take care of that,' Lucas said. 'Get yerself in the warm. Ain't there somewhere you can go?'

They were slow with shock and effort, and the question hung between them for a time.

'Married daughter . . . East Ham way.' The old man shifted and settled. 'I can go there.'

'The kid . . . who is she?' Lucas felt unable to take himself off until he knew she was being cared for.

The answer came after another pause. 'Annie? She and her ma had the basement in our house. I was just coming home – Christ!' He seemed to be willing the heap of bricks and mortar back in place, and when it didn't move he sighed heavily. 'Poor little sod. We'll see her right.'

Lucas took his clothes from the old man and put them on, noticing the soreness of his skin for the first time. 'I'll be off then.'

The old man took hold of his arm. 'Not till you've had a cupper tea or somethink stronger. They've a tea urn on the go at Juke's warehouse down the street – you need it. Might even get a bite to eat.'

All Lucas wanted was to be alone, but aware of utter fatigue, reluctantly allowed the old man to lead him down the shattered street to the shelter of the warehouse.

Every bone in Lucas's body ached, every muscle, every nerve. To make matters worse he was frozen to the marrow and his chest and hands were painfully sore. He rolled up in the nest of scavenged newspapers he had made. Now that the first drugged sleep of sheer exhaustion was over he knew in a muzzy way that the bitter cold would win. He fought to get back into dark oblivion, but half-dreams of the shattered body he had seen got in the way. With a grunt of disgust, he got up – muscles crying out – and shuffled across to the door of the derelict bakery, opening it just a crack to sniff the outside world. The noises that came were distant; the smells diluted. Golden Street slept. He closed the crack and leaned against the door, staring into the darkness. Somewhere along the way he had lost the daytime. It must be more than twenty-four hours since he was with Lil and Admiral in the kitchen, and then with Bella at the school. The tea and bread in between was a fading memory and there were hunger pains like screwdrivers boring into his stomach. Dreams of freedom, dreams of stone and statues would never be realized unless he faced the problem of how to stay alive and free. The time for indecision was past.

'Who's there?'

The door from the kitchen opened. Lily stood candle in hand, its light making strange ridges and pits out of her pudgy face. Lucas swore to himself, trying to shrink into the shadows at the end of the short passage. To have remained hidden all this time, even when the Admiral had come to bolt the back door before going to bed, and now to be discovered just because he'd had to ease his cramped leg and so made a noise, was enough to make a saint puke!

'Luke?' She peered at him. 'It is you, Luke?' holding the candle high. 'My Gawd, what happened?'

He had forgotten what he must look like with the mud and filth of Silvertown still clinging to clothes and hands – face too, more than likely, though he had tried to wipe it with rag and spit. Not bothering to answer, he pushed past her into the darkened kitchen. The fire was still glowing and he crouched by it shaking with cold.

'I'll fetch Bella,' Lily said. 'She's been worried sick. We all have. She told us what happened ... daft buggers. They've got no more sense in their heads than a flea with earache ... less!'

'No, don't.'

'Whyever not?'

'There's no point. I've just come to collect some bits, then I'll be off.' Weariness weighed on him. He couldn't deal with fuss.

'Luke Knight, you can't arrive out of the blue when we've all been worried to death and Bella going round like as if you'd died, and then take yerself off again without so much as a word.'

He straightened up, resenting the way she was making him feel guilty, and put out a hand. 'Here, give us a lend of the candle.'

She gave it to him and he went into the scullery, searching along the shelf, helping himself to a covered basin, then opening the stone crock and taking a knob end of loaf. Lily followed him. She was staring and obviously on the brink of a lot more words. He gave back the candle and took the spoils into the kitchen and began devouring congealed barley soup and bread; too hungry to bother with warming it.

'Well?' She stood over him, apparently waiting for an answer before setting about him.

He mopped up the last of the soup, cramming the bread into his mouth. 'Bella asleep?'

'I doubt it. Like a caged tiger she's been. Up and down the stairs all hours of the night.'

He looked at her, wondering if she had moved in permanently? Perhaps it would be a good thing if she had. Company for Bella and the old man. They'd always got along well. For himself he'd never been able to stand the way she always made a melodrama out of everything. The image of Bella as a caged tiger was stupid. He got up, pushing back the kitchen stool.

'I'll look in and see if she's awake when I've got me things.'

She moved in front of him, blocking the way. 'That ain't a ha'porth of good. I know you from a little lad – say one thing do another. Devious. No, I ain't getting ratty! I wouldn't dream of trying to argue you out of anythink you've set yer mind on. It's yer own business. But when it comes to mucking up other people's lives ... that's different. You saw the front door.'

He had been about to push her out of the way, but stopped. 'No?'

She gave a snort. 'Some dozy bugger's scrawled HUN LOVERS in red paint.'

The injustice stunned him. A man from this house was already fighting ... had been fighting for months and months! For three days only he had refused to go ... *three days*! Christ ... people! They got in the way all the time. If only he could live in a cave by the sea. Miles from anywhere or anybody. He shut his eyes tight. When he opened them, Bella was standing by the door at the bottom of the stairs.

'I knew you were here.' She came towards him, hugging the tatty old blanket she'd wrapped round herself. 'I'm that glad yer back safe. Where *have* you been? Y'look like a mudlark. Sit down. There's some soup I can warm. Won't take a tick.' There was a quiver in her voice but she valiantly held herself in check and was rewarded by a slow reluctant smile which spread across Lucas's face.

'I should've known there'd be no fooling you ... but yer too late for the soup. I've scoffed the lot.' It was uncanny the way she could sense his presence. In a lesser way he understood unspoken things about her, but never took much notice. Perhaps he ought to show her more concern, though it was probably too late. He might not see her again for months – if ever. The thought pierced him and made him surly. The opposite of what he wanted. 'I only came to fetch a few bits and pieces. Didn't mean to rouse the neighbourhood.'

'Where d'you intend going?' Lily asked, moving in like a battleship.

'It's best you shouldn't know.'

'Why d'you say that?'

'You can't talk about what you don't know.' He hadn't meant to be so cutting. It was only the truth after all.

'Are you suggesting I'd grass on you?' Lily said with some heat.

'You said it, not me.'

'Well of all the nerve ...'

Bella listened to them with growing exasperation until she could bear it no longer. 'Shut up,' she said loudly, and in the following lull: 'Scrapping's no answer.' She looked at Luke. 'There ain't too many things you can do to stay free, if yer still determined. Most of 'em need help. I'll help. And Lily ... if yer civil. We do care what happens to you, but we have to know. We can't work blind.' Her good intentions about remaining calm were slipping away with the stress of trying to convince him. She had hold of his jacket and when he tried to shake her off hung on with limpet strength. 'I must *know*. Yer mad, but if I'm not to end up in the loony bin alongside you, I've got to know what yer planning.'

'To get to the country somewhere,' he said evasively.

'Where *exactly*?'

Too tired to argue any more, Lucas gave in. 'Epping Forest – somewhere that way. Where we went that time with the Sunday School outing. There's plenty of places to hide out.'

'And you'll live on air I suppose,' she said tartly, then relented, knowing his fatigue as if it were her own. 'Look, why don't you go to Sylvia's place . . . in the Old Ford Road? She don't hold with conscription either and she knows people in the N-CF.'

'The what?'

'No-Conscription Fellowship.' At least she'd got his attention. 'You'd get a night's rest and perhaps a bit of a breather while you sorts things out with her. She won't turn you away.' He was hesitating, but definitely interested and she coaxed: 'I'll come with you if you likes. Emily Palmer . . . this girl I works with . . . she used to be a Suffragette. Knows the Pankhursts. It 'ud be an introduction.' The huge guesses were worth a try. Somebody had to keep their feet on the ground.

'All right,' Lucas said. 'I'll just make up a bundle.'

Heart singing, Bella ran up the stairs, happy to have found some sort of solution. The Admiral prevented her from doing what she had really wanted, which was to hide Luke at home, but this was a good second best.

Left alone in the kitchen, Lily stood for a moment before searching under the ample folds of her long skirt to find the hidden pocket. Then with two half-crowns and a tanner ready in her hand, she sat down in the Admiral's rocking chair and prepared to wait.

It was very dark. The wind had an edge to it that scythed through their clothes, and carried an acrid stench of burning, making Bella wrinkle her nose and hunch further into her clothes. The house in Old Ford Road looked blank and unlit. Not surprising at this time of night, but it didn't encourage her to knock. Nevertheless she must do so – she glanced back at Lucas hidden in the shadows of a nearby doorway – for his sake she must.

The first tentative tap produced nothing but an increase in the rate of her heartbeats. The second was bolder ... much bolder. Please don't let the neighbours hear and get nosy!

Light glimmered through the window and Bella heard someone moving about. Bolts were drawn, a key turned and the door opened a crack.

'Yes? Who is it?'

'Is Miss Pankhurst in? I must see her. It's urgent.'

'Can't it wait? It ain't exactly the time for visiting.' The whispering voice was faintly reproving.

'I know that and ... and I'm sorry, but it's an emergency. I ain't got nowhere else to turn.' What would she do if the woman shut the door in her face?

But the question didn't need an answer, because the door opened wider revealing a little woman with a large nose and grey hair plaited into a thin pigtail; a coat over her nightdress. Her eyes rounded in surprise and she said: 'Mercy!' then recovering herself: 'Sylvia ain't here, but you'd better come in. No point in filling the place full of draughts.'

Concealed in the doorway, Lucas watched Bella hesitate and look towards him before going inside. As the door closed behind her, he felt suddenly very alone. The future was menacing. He tried to wait patiently, but by the time she finally came out again, he had almost convinced himself that he ought to be on his way. Epping Forest was not so far. The difficulty lay in getting there without being accosted. London was full of patriots as well as bobbies and army police – all of them waiting to pounce.

Bella was beckoning. Go or stay? The ability to make any proper decision had temporarily deserted him and he took the easy way out, reluctantly crossing the pavement.

'Sylvia ain't home,' she told him in a breathy whisper. 'But this lady says she knows someone who'll help. A Mrs West. She's set against the war and has given a hand to more than one on the run.'

He nodded, fatigue overwhelming him. He wasn't at all happy about the way things had been taken out of his control, but to rebel would call on reserves of energy he hadn't got.

Bella went on: 'You should be safe enough for tonight and tomorrow. After that ...' she let the suggestion that it was up to him come without words, as if it was something she couldn't bear to say. 'Dunno how long you'll be able to stay, but it's the best we can do for now. I can't come no further. Lily'll be waiting and Grandad might wake ... besides, I've got to be at work tomorrow. I daren't miss ... daren't let there be any questions.'

He knew by the roughness of her voice and the hasty way she spoke that she was screwed up tight inside. He felt pretty rocky himself. This was the point when their ways divided. The first real parting of their lives, because the last few weeks when he'd lived at the workshop didn't count. She was standing in a curiously stiff attitude as if holding herself together. A peg doll – he thought.

The little woman who was to be his guide said anxiously: 'We shouldn't oughter dawdle.'

'Luke!' Bella launched herself at him with a fierceness that took him by surprise. He was moved and shaken by the closeness of her which said all the things words could not, and kissed her, hugging her briefly before unlocking her arms, so that he could walk away. He didn't look back because it was too painful, and because with her uncanny way of guessing his mood she might sense his relief that the waiting was over.

8

'I've brought you a cupper tea, young feller. No point in wasting a fresh pot.'

Lucas rolled over on the lumpy sofa and stared at the elderly woman looking down on him. His eyes took in the square shape of her, but his mind, still wading through dreams, enlarged her to giant size. Her head was a distant mask that grinned, revealing a graveyard; the skin netted over with fine wrinkles. And then reality fell on him. Mrs West. Mrs West's sofa. Mrs West's back room where the little woman had brought him the night before.

'You been sleeping like the dead,' Mrs West said.

Not a giant, but built like a navvy. Twice as broad as he was and a head taller. Would have been taller still but for years of toil that had curved her shoulders and back.

'What time is it?' Lucas sat up and took the mug, warming his hands.

'Quarter to eleven.' She chuckled at his astonishment. 'I been up for hours. Just looked in now to tend the fire and make a drink. Got up this mornin', raked the ashes, built the fire, brewed up, got me breakfast, washed the pots. You slept through the lot.'

A triangle of sunlight edged in through the narrow window behind him and changed a wedge of her black skirt to dingy green, picking out individual fibres on part of her sacking apron. The room around was sparsely furnished and brown. It might have been different once, but now only the fire in the freshly blacked range had any sparkle. He sniffed the left-behind scent of fried bread, and felt truly famished, but reminded himself sternly that he must learn to live with hunger.

As if she understood his thoughts, Mrs West cut two doorsteps of bread from the loaf on the table, then moved a heavy iron frying pan over the flames. 'Lottie's looking after the shop for me. She s a good gal. She won't ask no questions.'

He knew the shop was the shed at the end of the yard. Once a coalhouse, it had been scrubbed, whitewashed and given a counter. A wide variety of goods was sold there, from liquorice root right the way through bootlaces, beeswax and firewood to secondhand clothes and coal. The coal was piled outside. The sacks in a heap at the back of the shop. The little woman had explained everything on the way here the night before.

Mrs West arranged the golden bread on a plate crazed with brown cracks, topped it with some crispy bits of bacon fat, and made a place for him at the table. 'Get that inside you, then we can talk.'

Lucas obeyed, gratefully accepting a second mug of tea.

'Now then ... to get down to brass tacks. I been told yer aiming to get out of London going north. Can't help you all the way – even if I knew where, which I don't *and* don't want to. But it just so happens that I promised me Auntie I'd take her a couple o' sacks o' coal. She lives Stratford way. Cleans for Mr Mabel the cold cook, or did before the pneumony made him one of his own customers. Now his missus runs the business, and Auntie gives her a hand with the laying out as well. Got quite a way with it she has.'

Several thoughts whipped simultaneously through Lucas's head as she paused for a mouthful of tea. He was relieved at her lack of curiosity, but alarmed at the idea of going anywhere in broad daylight with or without a sack of coal. And what delivery cart? The only vehicle he'd seen around was that old pram. A pram full of coals being pushed along by a fit young bloke, and a darkie at that, would be a prime target for any bobby.

'Heard of the N-CF?' Mrs West looked at him from under the ledges where her eyebrows should have been.

He blinked – the question taking a moment to register. 'A bit. Not much.'

'A bunch of toffs as think like you. At least, they ain't all toffs. Some of 'em are yer sort . . . well almost. Sylvia told me about 'em first, when young Ted . . .' She broke off and swallowed more tea. 'But that's another story. Had enough, young feller? I could do you one more slice.'

'No thanks.' Lucas had decided to discipline himself, guessing he had already made substantial inroads into her meagre food store. 'But if there's any tea left?'

She took his mug. 'I can get you as far as Auntie's no trouble. Bit more tricky from her house to Mabel's, but a hundred yards shouldn't be more than a smart young cove like yerself can manage. You'll be safe enough there – until things is fixed.'

Lucas was lost. Seeing his bewilderment, another bout of chuckling shook her, expanding until she clutched her ribs.

'I can just see . . . oh mercy . . . you . . . oh me stays . . . stretched out . . .' she punched his shoulder, then wiped her streaming eyes. 'Oh my . . .'

He was still in the dark and she said more collectedly: 'Think, young feller. Use yer grey matter. What's Mabel's business?'

'Undertakers,' Lucas said.

'And what's an undertaker's stock in trade?'

'Corpses.'

'And corpses go in . . .'

'Coffins.' Christ, she didn't mean . . .

Mrs West nodded. 'Got it! Yer a shortie so there shouldn't be no trouble fitting you up. Room for yer bits an' all.'

He was to lie in a coffin. Blotted from the light. For how long and for what purpose? Having helped in the making of coffins he knew that even the roughest job would be impossible for him to break from without help. A thin sweat raised on his face and worked down his body.

'Better to lie in one living than dead, darlin',' Mrs West said kindly, leaning across the table and briefly squeezing his arm. It was like being clamped in a vice wrapped in old scaly leather.

Even so; even if the lid was only lodged . . . He shivered.

Mrs West stood up. 'I must get back to the shop. Lottie's

got to go on an errand for her ma before dinner. We'll be off to Auntie's this afternoon. I can close up. Not much doing of a Sunday anyway.'

He watched her collect the greasy plate and mugs. There was a soothing calm about her, but he couldn't fathom why she was bothering with a total stranger, because that's what he was. The enigma was why she was taking such a serious risk to help *him*.

'Why d'you do it? They could nick you an' all if they found me here. No two ways.'

'I likes to help when I can.'

'But why? I ain't nothink to you.'

She paused, lodging the pile of crockery between her belly and the edge of the table. 'Me son's the reason. Oh not what yer thinking. Nothink to do with the war. It was a long time ago. He was a bit soft in the head . . . nothink I couldn't manage. But they said I wasn't able to care for him proper on account of having to go out to work. Didn't have the shop then y'see. He liked a bit o' freedom did Harry. Used to roam and folk didn't always understand when he helped himself to an apple or an orange. Didn't know about paying y'see. Once he took a glass necklace just because it was shiny.' She raised her shoulders and let them fall again. 'So they shut him up. First the nick then the loony bin. He died there. *He* liked *his* freedom, see?' She crossed to the tin basin on a washstand by the range and put the dirty pots in it, then lifted the kettle from the hob.

A bit of a joke the way death was to save him from death at every turn. He asked tentatively: 'D'you mean me to push the coal barrer?'

'Lor love yer no! I'll push *you*.'

For one fantastic minute he saw himself in a frilled bonnet, legs dangling over the end of the rickety pram. Then she said:

'You'll fit in one o' them coal sacks snug as a bug. Lucky yer such a lean 'un.'

It was cool in the long outbuilding at the back of Mabel's, but not unbearably so, and the friendly snuffles and stamping of the three horses in their stalls was heartening. Lucas had always liked horses, especially the great Percherons pulling brewery drays. They provided colour, majesty, huge shapes thudding along the roads.

He looked round.

Beyond the stalls – two hearses. One elegant; ornate. Frosted scrolls and lilies patterning the glass. Bodywork as black and gleaming as beeswax and elbow grease could make it. Interior a rich expanse of sooty velvet. The other was more workaday – 'For customers as are hard pushed' Auntie said. Beyond these, the old converted piano cart used to collect the dead. Beyond again, coffins layered up the wall. A poor enough business even with the extra horses hired from a job-master when needed, as were the mourning coaches.

And Auntie herself. Massive as her niece and much the same age. 'Her ma and me were opposite ends of twelve kids,' she had told him in one of the brief times she had spent with him during the day and night at her lodgings. Most of his stay had been solitary, with only lowering thought for company.

The thoughts were with him still.

He moved closer to one of the living, breathing, sharp-smelling horses – a dark sturdy cob called Barley – rubbing its velvet nose; being gently lipped in return; getting up courage to examine the coffin; his coffin – already in place inside the piano cart. For today was the day. Any moment he would be laid out, being driven by Auntie – whose skills were apparently endless – some way beyond the Jews' Cemetery where he was to get out and make his way to 13 East Grove Avenue, the home of Mr Graham, a Quaker and member of the N-CF.

'A gent with his finger in a lot of pies. Knows all kinds. Helped others like yerself out of London, and more. His house is only a stone's throw from me customer's. Shouldn't be no trouble if you walks nice and brisk. Tell him as I sent you. I'll try and get a message to him by the lad beforehand so as he'll be expecting you.'

He had listened to the plummy voice, fascinated by her confidence and the way her chins wobbled as she spoke. Her tightly pinned hair was a peppery colour and reminded him of a cat Bella had rescued from the canal when she was a kid. She treated his escape as if it were an everyday occurrence, and her composure was amazing. But even so he couldn't shake off the feeling that the coming journey was make-believe – part of this Picture Palace stuff Bella lapped up. Even now, with the coffin under his nose, he couldn't quite believe he'd agreed to take part. The more he thought, the more fantastic the idea became.

He went to the piano cart. There was the coffin. *His* coffin. Repressing a shudder, he made himself explore the lid with his fingers to get rid of the nightmare feeling by studying the thing with a professional eye. His hand progressing to the coffin itself, he ran a thumb down one joint. A poor job. He felt slightly put out, both for himself and for the soldier whose last resting place this was to be. Neither of them had any choice. He experienced the rough wooden surface with the flat of his hand. A very poor job indeed.

The clatter and creak coming from the street lost importance as his ears registered the scrape of hob-nailed boots crossing the courtyard. There was no more time for doubts.

'Get in y'great soft 'nana,' he muttered to himself. 'It's only planks of wood!'

Balancing the lid at an angle between coffin side and cart roof, he eased his bundle then himself through the aperture. Auntie had said she would slot the lid in place, but the sound of those boots wasn't quite right. He couldn't afford to take chances. Slowly he lowered the lid.

Darkness smacked across his face. All sounds immediately muffled. Everywhere the strong clean smell of planed elm. He'd known it would be unpleasant, cramped, even stifling, but had told himself it was another discipline to be accepted and would not last. What he hadn't anticipated was rising rebellious panic at the thick blackness that pressed in. This life-long fear of blindness almost undid him. But things began to happen.

'Whoa, Barley ... come along now ... that's it, gal ... bit more ... and again.'

A kid's voice. The lad. He'd been right to trust his ears.

The scuffling metallic noise of Barley's hooves echoed dully into the wooden prison. There was a jolt. And another. Backwards. Forwards again. Barley being harnessed to the piano cart. Keep down y'fool! No grabbing at fresh air and light.

'Everything all right, Joey?' Auntie's rich voice, puffing with exertion.

'Right as a winkle on a pin, missus.'

The cart rolled forward, bumping and rocking.

Half an hour. No time at all. An eternity. Think about how to hop it unseen, while Auntie and the lad were inside the house 'trimming up the stiff' as she put it. There was a small lane up the back where the cart would be stationed, with a one in ten chance of nosy parkers. Who was he kidding! Accidents, death, anything with the least inkling of drama drew folk like wasps to jam. And coffins were big drama. Christ, he'd never get away. He never should've listened. Never fallen into this nightmare.

The rattle and judder as the cart jogged along dropped into a pattern that Lucas found he could interpret. Every now and again the shaking would be less rapid and the neat clop clop of Barley's hooves changed to a muffled scraping as Auntie reigned him in when traffic thickened. Smells seeped in. The hot sour-sweetness of washing being boiled; the oily sharpness of petrol; a whiff of burnt coffee; sweet fragrance from a bakery. He seized and held them, working hard to map out the history of the journey so there would be no time nor thought for panic. It was like walking the rim of a volcano. Once the cart stopped with a jerk and there was a buzz of angry voices. Once they swayed round a corner and the coffin began to side-slip. Lucas sweated. The seconds stretched out; became minutes, hours, weeks ... A jolt and they were bowling along steadily now with elm wood the strongest smell. He hung on to himself, fighting down the irresistible urge to push up the coffin lid and escape.

The sounds altered subtly; the metallic crunching of the wheels changing to a thick padded rumble as they swivelled right then left; coffin slithering. It was no more than an inch or two each time, but the sensation underlined his helplessness. He couldn't take much more.

The cart halted. Stillness hit him, then was shattered again as the whole structure shook – Auntie clambering from her seat. Lucas let out a great sigh of relief and, putting the flat of his hands against the coffin lid, pushed.

Oh the blessed glorious light! The intensity of it was almost painful, making him squint, but he refused to shut his eyes. It didn't matter a toss that the sky was a lid of heavy grey. *He wasn't blind any more!*

The crack became a chasm of brilliance.

'Quick as you can.' Auntie was propping the coffin lid against the side of the cart. 'I've sent the lad round to the front door. There ain't much time.'

Lucas sat up, hotching forward till he could drape his legs over the end of the coffin. 'Thanks ... but I don't never want to do that again!'

'Let's hope you only need it the once more.'

With a heave and a scramble he was standing on the packed earth of a narrow entry dividing the back gardens of two rows of terraced houses. Windows were at a small distance and there were several large bushes and two lime trees for shelter. He rescued his bundle.

'Hurry ... don't hang about.' Auntie slid the coffin lid back in place with an expertise born of much practice.

Lucas offered his hand. 'I shan't forget. Straight up!'

She took it in a horny grip. 'Good luck, young 'un ... now git on with you.'

The first patter of rain arrived with Lucas at the end of the entry. He paused briefly under an overhanging holly bush to get his bearings. The main road was to the left and this he must cross, angling left again because East Grove Avenue lay parallel behind it. The rain was gathering power, bouncing on the road in individual fountains as a woman came out of the pinched Gothic house opposite, pausing to put up her umbrella. She looked full at him. Lucas turned up his collar and tucking his bundle more securely under his arm stepped out with purpose. The last thing he wanted was to be remembered as a loiterer. The colour of his skin was badge enough to mark him out.

Traffic was thin as he crossed the road. A bicycle splashed past. People had their heads down or were sheltering in shop doorways gazing at the sky. Nobody watched him and – greatest relief of all – no bobbies were in sight. Rain, penetrating and cold, was trickling down his neck now, but his mouth and throat were desert dry. A tempting pub called the Three Hands stood on the corner of the side street he was to take. A beer-soaked haven. Snug and taproom would be smoky warm. A place to quench his thirst and let the rain steam from his clothes.

He walked on through the downpour.

East Grove Avenue was a hotchpotch of buildings dominated by a Methodist chapel of brash red brick which fronted the pavement. Further on a row of respectable villas sat back with small apron lawns and dripping privet hedges. Number thirteen boasted a cluster of laurel bushes huddling close to the porch. Unlatching the gate, Lucas went boldly up the path, knocked and waited.

He waited three minutes. Four. Ten. Knocking at intervals.

The truth stared at him bleakly. Nobody was there. Bella's efforts, Mrs West's, her Auntie's, the coffin journey ... all for nothing! As if to put a stamp on his predicament the rain changed to a gusty drizzle blown by a thin cutting wind which diluted his feeling of purpose and watered down his common sense, leaving him dithering over whether to wait even longer or cut his losses and start walking. While he was hesitating the front door of the neighbouring house clicked open and an elderly woman's face appeared. Small owl eyes blinked through tortoiseshell spectacles and a prim voice asked:

'Were you looking for Mr Graham?'

Lucas said: 'Yes,' before he had time to calculate the wisdom of admitting it.

'Fetched this morning he was. Him and the other gentleman. Hasn't been back since.'

'Fetched?' He felt a tingle of alarm.

'Yes. The police came.'

The bobbies! It was crackers asking, but he had to know why. Had to be certain.

'They didn't give a reason.' The owl eyes blinked slowly, then crinkled up. She seemed to be fixing him in her memory. 'Of course I know what I *think*, but it wouldn't do to say.'

Lucas knew what he thought too, but wasn't given time to act on it.

'You're one of them.' Not a question but a statement.

'Me ... no!' He knew, despairingly, that he had been too emphatic.

'Stands to reason,' she went on relentlessly. 'Well set-up young fellow like yourself, out of khaki.'

'No. It's not ... I came for ... somethink else.' He left the porch, sidling down the path. 'Thanks ... I'll ... thanks ...' Aware that he had stayed far too long, he hurried towards the gate and the street. There was nothing for it but to do what he should have done in the first place. Depend on himself.

Having made that decision, the next was less obvious. Walking on a fine night and in dry clothes would have no problems, bar the risk of being accosted. Walking on a filthy night like this and soaked to the skin was a different matter altogether. Dying of exposure was no part of his plan.

Of course there was the pub ...

Or the chapel ...

He settled for the chapel – a cold dark place, but dry – and went in. Choosing a spot behind the harmonium as the only possible hiding place, he did what he could to make himself comfortable. During this time an old woman came in, shuffled up the aisle, selected a chair and knelt down on the hassock in front of it. Cold and still as the tiles on which he sat, Lucas waited. Then his leg went to sleep and he was forced to move. The sounds he made exploded on the silence, but the old woman was apparently hard of hearing. She was also a believer in lengthy prayers.

The bang of a door and scrape of a turning key woke Lucas from an uneasy doze. He uncurled his aching limbs, groping from behind the harmonium. No need for caution now. He almost ran to the heavy mahogany door at the far end, twisting the ring handle and pushing.

Gawd streuth he was locked in! How was he going to get out? And how long had he been here?

A window in the vestry was large enough to squeeze through and he found himself in a favourably dim secluded yard. But the door leading to the street was locked. Abandoning caution he followed his bundle over the wall like a trained gymnast, dropping into the street. He had only one thought – at all costs he must get warm and reasonably dry if he was to spend the night in the open. It was the pub or nothing.

A stone's throw from the pub doors he paused, gathering his courage. He could hear a banjo playing 'Little Grey Home in the West', towing a group of voices. Through the window came the warm pub glow, lighting squares of coloured glass. He took a deep breath and opened the door. Beery song and a wonderful fug flowed out, wrapping round him. Inside, he glanced quickly round the room. Bar and fireplace were crowded. The banjo player was perched on a high stool close to the fire and had paused to take a swig of beer and mop his face. Lucas eased towards the bar and waited to catch the attention of the barmaid, but before he did, a couple of soldiers squeezed in beside him. They were already well-oiled and were arguing.

'... nothing but a bloody cog in a machine, mate. Like we all are. Ain't my fault now is it?' The soldier speaking appealed to the whole bar, his glassy gaze coming to rest on Lucas while his clipped moustache underlining his beaky nose bristled and twitched. The other – short, stocky with untamed sandy eyebrows – took off his cap and scratched his head.

‘Ye know how to spin a wee tale, I’ll grant ye that,’ he said in a considerable Scots accent.

Lucas tried to catch the barmaid’s eye, hoping to get a drink quickly then slither away. But she ignored him and the thin soldier took hold of his arm.

‘Less have another ’pinion. You listen now ... thiss bugger says iss my fault I ain’t done a stint at the Front. Now I asks you, how c’n that be true?’

There was a grim humour about the question, only Lucas wasn’t in a laughing mood. He tried to smile in a non-committal way and made another vain attempt to get some service.

The Scot elbowed his mate. ‘Know how to work your ticket, thass how. Cushy number ye’ve got for yersel’.’

‘Cushy number! Hear that?’ Clipped moustache hung on to Lucas’s arm so it was impossible to get away without causing trouble. At the back of the bar was a plate-glass mirror reflecting everything behind – people, the fluted opal of the hanging gas-light; the wall and picture of ‘Blind Hope’; the door opening.

‘Bleedin’ ’ell,’ Lucas’s captor went on, shaking him. ‘Y’should try being an arms insh–instructor. Bloody burks firing all over the shop. Miracle if any of ’em makes the target. Couldn’t hit’n elephant’s arse at point-blank range.’ He swayed slightly, using Lucas to steady himself. ‘’Sright, ain’t it mate?’

But Lucas wasn’t paying any attention. He was looking in the mirror, watching the progress of two policemen who had come in. They shut the door and scanned the room.

The Scot bristled. ‘Ye bloody dare to stand there and say us Jocks can’t shoot shtraight? Bloody ask Fritz then.’

The bobbies were going from table to table, asking questions, moving inevitably towards the bar. The woman had shopped him and he would never get away. He was trapped and without a chance of a drink or a warm.

‘Didn’t say that did I?’ The soldier was clinging with both hands now. ‘But y’d be in a fix if there weren’t anyone t’show y’in the firs’ place ... thass what I’m saying.’

Lucas tried to pull away. He saw one of the policemen look

full at him in the mirror and he saw himself – a lump of coal in a basket of eggs. A dead ringer! These bobbies had never had an easier job!

'Aw go on!' the Scot said. 'Have 'nother drink and keep y'hair on or ...' He stopped, catching sight of the policeman, and turned round.

'Here ... you!' The policeman leaned over and put a large hand on Lucas's shoulder. 'We want a word with you.'

Now that the moment had arrived, Lucas felt his despair being replaced by a strange sense of relief. Everyone was looking at him, but it didn't matter any more. The time for hiding was over, and he was glad because there never had been anywhere to go. Whatever was to come would be real.

9

'GET in there!'

Lucas was shoved roughly through the open door into the harsh light of the police station. Then shoved again, sending him knocking against the reception desk. The sergeant behind it scowled.

'Here you! What d'you think yer playing at?' He swivelled his globular eyes from the papers he was checking, taking in first Lucas, then the constable behind him. His grizzled eyebrows twitched up.

'Got a deserter here, Sarge. Had this tip-off and found him skulking in the Three Hands.' The statement was accompanied by painful prodding under Lucas's shoulder-blade.

'Well, well, well!' The sergeant's thick eyebrows met in a line and his voice hardened. 'Deserter eh? A funky little coward.'

'I'm not a deserter,' Lucas said.

The sergeant smiled coldly, his white even false teeth showing up with uncanny brilliance against a spreading iron-grey moustache and the paler grey patchiness of his skin. 'Prove it then.' His upper set dropped from his gums and then clicked back. 'Go on, let's see yer papers . . . yer leave pass, sonny.'

'He ain't got any, Sarge. I've checked.'

'I'm not a deserter,' Lucas repeated, hoping they couldn't see how much he was shaking.

The sergeant sniffed. 'If yer not, then either yer a furriner – which could be, though you don't sound it,' he considered Lucas inch by inch, 'or yer a loony. Whichever, we'll soon find out.' He picked up a pen from a small tray on the desk and dipped it in the inkwell. 'Name and address?'

'Lucas Knight . . .' he hesitated, not wanting to say where he lived for Bella's sake, and the Admiral's.

'Address I said. Gone deaf have you?'

What was the use? He was caught. Now or in a week or two weeks they would know everything about him. There was no point in trying to cover up.

'Poplar. Golden Street, Poplar,' he said wearily.

'*Golden Street!*' The sergeant laughed mockingly. 'Hear that, Baxter? *Golden* Street . . . and him like a burnt cinder! How old are you, Sonny Jim?'

'Seventeen,' Lucas lied with sudden inspiration.

'He never is. He never said that before, Sarge. Not when I arrested him, nor on the way here. Constable Jones was with me. He'll vouch that's true.'

'Liar into the bargain are you?' The sergeant paused in his writing and leaned towards him. His breath was sour, but Lucas could not back away, trapped as he was between the desk and the bulk of Constable Baxter. 'I want proper answers – no lies. Now . . . what's the number of your house?'

'Nineteen.'

'Parents have you? Brothers? Sisters?'

'One brother. One sister. Me parents is dead.'

'Lucky for them I'd say, because if yer of age and not a cripple or a loony then they'd be properly shamed.'

Lucas shut his eyes.

'Why ain't you in the army?'

Words were no good. Whatever he said they'd never believe him; never understand. They were already against him. He could feel it.

'Answer when yer spoke to!' The gimlet finger was jabbing his back again. He opened his eyes.

'I . . . I don't want to join up.'

'Don't *want*?' The sergeant coughed and a wind of stale breath puffed into Lucas's face. 'What d'you mean "don't want"? What's wanting or not wanting got to do with it? It's yer duty, lad. You should look on it as an honour to be able to defend yer country.'

'That ain't the way I sees it. War's wrong.' Lucas began to sweat. He'd spoken out now. There was no retreat.

'My Gawd, it's another of them bloody conchies you've brought in, Baxter. And a nigger at that. A bloody nigger with the gall ... the bloody nerve ...' he searched for words as if such audacity had swept his memory clean away. His face blotched and Lucas saw how his hand tightened on the pen. The air seemed to fill with threat as if violence was simmering close to the surface and any moment would burst through. But all that happened was that the sergeant put down his pen and came round in front of the desk.

'Conchie are you?'

'Yes.'

'Aaah!' The sighing breath was like odours escaping from rotting vegetables. 'You don't look like one of them Quakers.'

'I ain't.'

'What are you then? Seventh Day Adventist? Pillar of Fire?'

'No. Nothink like that.'

There was a quivering pause. The grey face came very close.

'There's got to be some reason, sonny. Or are you plain scared?' The contempt softened a little. 'A lot of men are scared at first, but it don't keep them from their duty. They ain't shirkers. They act like men and a lot of 'em die like men.'

There was nothing to say. No answer that was the slightest use.

The sergeant cuffed his shoulder with a sudden sharp movement, making him fall back against the constable who immediately pushed him away. The sergeant cuffed him again, painfully, with a clenched fist.

'Yer Country Needs You. Know that poster? Know it?' His voice was harsh now and he shoved Lucas against Baxter for the second time, who returned the shove. Lucas wondered how long he was to be batted between them.

'Come on now – d'you know it?'

'Yes.'

'Kitchener. Field Marshal he was. A Field Marshal telling you yer duty. Now then, what d'you say? Answer the call like a man, sonny, and there'll be no more trouble.' The sergeant's voice had changed from threat to appeal, leaving Lucas bewildered.

'You'll never get this little squirt to act sensible, Sarge,' Baxter said scornfully.

'He should have a second chance. Everyone makes mistakes sometimes. I knows it ain't easy, but you've got no choice really, sonny – gaol or firing squad or army.'

Lucas had no way of knowing if this was the truth, but on the surface it seemed likely. It was a terrible choice and no choice.

'I can't do what ain't right.' It was all he could say. He became aware of a sudden feeling of great strength which seemed to come from deep inside. He felt glowing and strangely calm. He knew that after all, whatever happened, somehow he would be able to hang on and not betray his intense belief in what it meant to be alive and to know beauty. These were the great gifts; to squander them was worse than a crime ... unthinkable. He looked at the two men and saw plainly that no ordinary explanation would make sense.

The sergeant's fist bunched and Lucas heard his scandalized voice say: '*Right? ...*' but was spared what might have come, as a small mouse-like woman scurried in, face flushed with distress. She came close to the sergeant, putting a shaking hand on his arm. Her voice was agitated.

'It's Freddie, Sergeant. He's gone for good this time. I know it. Vanished entirely. I've searched high and low ... under the stairs ...'

'One minute, Miss Mincher.' The sergeant covered her hand, but she would not be restrained.

'I'm so afraid he'll be run down. He doesn't understand about street dangers you see.'

The sergeant said: 'Have you tried next door?' The change in manner was startling – patient and sympathetic.

'Yes . . . yes of course.' Her voice rose and ended in a sob.

'Now don't you fret, m'dear. He'll turn up. Cats have nine lives.' He patted her hand and turned to Baxter. 'Take that scum down and lock him up. He's made his choice.'

The constable took Lucas through swing doors, along a passage, then down a flight of stairs to a cell in the basement, shoving him hard inside. He said with a hint of satisfaction:

'Made yer bed proper, ain't you? Well enjoy it. Yer here for as long as it takes.' The door slammed. A key rattled and was withdrawn.

For some moments Lucas remained where he was, facing the rough whitewashed bricks of the wall. Then slowly turned to face the door.

It fitted snugly into the surrounding wall. A small spy-hole was the only break in the smooth surface. There was no door-knob of any kind. No way to open it. No means of going out of his own free will. The horror of it hit him, leaving him weak and sick. He felt choked and leaned back against the wall, slowly slithering down until he was crouched knees to chest, holding his legs tight to him and burying his face away from the gaslight which hissed naked above the terrible door.

Sitting on the edge of the plank bed in the cell Lucas felt hot and feverish. Someone had given his throat a going over with a nutmeg grater and his eyeballs seemed achingly fat. The ache stretched into his bones and his damp clothes crawled over his skin. Overnight the cell had filled and another bed brought in. The raucous snores of the drunken old lush on it scratched his nerves. It would have been better to be alone. He looked at the bloke leaning against the wall picking his nose. He was bearable – but the other one, pacing up and down in a figure of eight, avoiding that stinking bucket each time – he was enough to drive a saint to drink. He'd been at it for hours.

'Why don't you take a pew, mate? There's room.' Lucas shifted along the plank.

The man paused, smiling faintly. 'I'd rather not if you don't mind. Thanks all the same.'

He sounded a bit of a posh geyser. Surprising and not surprising. Clothes shabby but fair quality. Nondescript somehow. Unguessable age as well. Lucas sneezed and searched for a handkerchief. It was damp like the rest of him and as he blew his nose a great depression settled. What a charlie he'd been! Made a proper muck. All that help and where had it got him? Locked up like a criminal and with a hatching cold. He would have shown more sense if he'd walked into a police station as soon as the call-up card came and told them straight. At least he'd be fit now. Gawd that bucket made a stench. He sneezed again.

'Grim place, isn't it?' The plank shook and creaked.

Lucas came out of his blind gloom to find the man beside him, having apparently changed his mind. From this angle his face had a curious twisted look, as if it had been sat on and pressed over to one side. His smile was also lop-sided and the whole effect reminded Lucas of an oddly shaped parsnip he'd once seen.

The man went on: 'Not what you'd call an hotel.'

Lucas was silent, knowing nothing of hotels except from the outside. He felt at a disadvantage.

'Just for one night though, I hope. Though I daresay there's worse to come. I'm up before the Magistrate tomorrow.'

'What you been nicked for?' Lucas asked.

'Which version do you want, the authority's or mine?'

Lucas considered. 'Both.'

'Ah, a man of perception.' The smile broadened, emphasizing the parsnip likeness. 'They say I'm a deserter. I say I am a socialist and as such don't recognize their authority to make me a soldier against my will.'

Lucas looked at him with renewed interest. 'You a conchie?'

'If you want to put it like that.'

There was a pause while Lucas digested this information. Here was a bloke who may have had some experience of what happened to conchies. A bloke to be questioned, and yet to do so would be to lay himself open. Instinct said keep quiet.

'And you?' the man asked after a period of silent observation.

Oh what the hell – he thought – I'm in the shit up to me eyeballs. Might as well learn all I can. 'Same reason as you ... well almost. I'm not a socialist,' whatever that might mean.

The smile was in danger of splitting the parsnip in two. Lucas found his hand being gripped and shaken warmly. 'What a pleasure this is. A friend. A fellow thinker. Tell me, what did you say to the Tribunal and what rubbish did they ask you? I suppose the Appeal turned you down as well?'

'Hold on a minute ... what's a Tribunal?' Lucas asked.

'You haven't been then? I don't understand. Why are you here? They generally let you stay home till after the hearing. You've had the form I presume?'

'If you mean the card telling me to report to the barracks – yes. I didn't wait to find out no more. Me mistake was needing a drink.'

'They took you in a pub?'

'That's right, but I never got me drink did I? This old girl I'd been gabbing to earlier shopped me and the bobbies turned up, and you can see for yerself how easy I am to find. So here we are. Dunno what's next.' He looked hopefully at this experienced rebel. 'Do you?'

The man laced his fingers and hooked both hands round his knees, bunching his shoulders and rocking. 'I can tell you the routine for most COs, but there's often a gap between what should happen and what does.'

'Well?'

'Most go in front of their local Tribunal – that's a group of local worthies appointed to listen to their objections to fighting. It's like a sort of trial. They decide yes or no. Mostly it's no, though some are lucky – they either get off or have the chance to settle for the Non-Combatant Corps – in the army but without carrying arms. They do things like repair roads and railways, see to sanitary arrangements, ambulance work, things like that.'

So it wasn't hopeless. He wouldn't mind road work or even cleaning the bogs now they'd actually caught him. He'd be able to keep quiet and out of trouble. Survive.

'After that,' the man went on, 'if it's been no twice – you're allowed to appeal you see – they call you up again. And if you still refuse, they put you in jug overnight, then when the Magistrate's fined you two quid the military takes over. You're carted off to the barracks you were supposed to go to in the first place. And after *that* . . .' he shrugged.

'It's been no for you?'

'Twice. But if it was a hundred times I wouldn't change.'

Lucas was filled with admiration. He wished some of the man's cheerful confidence would rub off on him and he thought – if he can stick it, I ought to. He said: 'They'll do for me all right. All I can tell 'em is I don't fancy getting killed or killing anybody else. It's such a waste. They'll die laughing I shouldn't wonder.' The earlier spark of hope had quickly been extinguished. He stared morosely at the dirty floor.

A hand rested on his shoulder. He felt the pressure and looked up, meeting the grey irregular eyes; finding an infinite depth of understanding and sympathy there. For once he didn't resent it. After all they were in the same boat.

'There's a lot of us,' the man said quietly. 'Whatever happens there's no need to feel alone even if you are in solitary. Heard of the No-Conscription Fellowship?'

'A bit. Not much.'

'A resistance movement, you might call it. Formed to protest . . . and look after chaps like us. D'you know they've got records of just about every CO in that little office of theirs?'

'Where's that?' Lucas asked.

'Oh, just off Fleet Street,' the man was vague, glancing at the silent prisoner propping up the wall. 'But you'll be on their lists don't you worry – once you've had your hearing.'

'How d'you know so much?' There seemed no end to the man's knowledge or his confidence.

'Because I've worked for them. Gathering information and selling the *Tribunal* ... that's their newspaper. Comic isn't it?' seeing Lucas's bewilderment. 'Well chosen though – the name I mean. Wish I'd got a copy to show you. I did bring one, but the sergeant out there confiscated it. Perhaps he'll read it and be converted. There's always hope!'

'Y'sniffin' dirty pair o' shirkers!' The man Lucas had earlier considered inoffensive had jerked away from the wall and was glowering down at them with a kind of dislocated venom. 'They've no business shutting the likes of you up with decent blokes. Sitting there rating yer chances of getting off scot free ... dunno how you've the bloody face. And you ...' He pointed at Lucas. 'You don't even belong here!'

Lucas's new acquaintance looked up. 'You're entitled to your opinion, friend,' he said mildly. 'But there's no need to be insulting.'

Under his greyish stubble the man's face mottled. 'It's you that's bloody insulting. I ain't yer friend ... bloody ponce!' He suddenly lunged forward, his fist smashing against the side of the young man's temple. Lucas saw his friend fall back against the wall and was on his feet grabbing at the man's arms to prevent him landing another punch, but was almost bowled over by the weight of his body. For a minute they wrestled, the man grunting and swearing. Lucas felt himself being forced backwards, legs pressing against the plank bed, and with a crash he collapsed, his arms pinioned by the body of the man who had fallen on top of him. He tried desperately to wriggle free, but couldn't. The man raised his fist but before he could deliver the blow, Lucas's friend gripped his arm and flung him on to his back.

The door of the cell swung open and a voice bellowed: 'What the bloody hell's going on in here?'

Lucas sat up and the other two scrambled to their feet facing the police sergeant.

'Come on then ... what happened?'

In the instant quiet of the cell, where even the snores of the drunk had been doused, the three men stared at the floor. Nobody spoke and the police sergeant glared round.

'We're all struck dumb then are we? All right. But if I hear so much as another squeak out of any of you, I'll blast you from here to the Somme. Understand?'

Still no sound or movement. A creak of boots, the door slammed, the key rattled in the lock.

Lucas sat down very still on the edge of the bed, trying to quieten the battlefield in his head. The steady throb reached across the top of his skull and down into the nape of his neck. But for all that he felt better than he had done all day, and recognized that the unexpected bust up had come as a relief.

The plank bed moved as his new friend came closer, whispering: 'Thanks,' in his ear.

Lucas looked at him, then at the other man propped scowling in a corner. 'For what?'

'Stepping in . . . lending a hand.' The long thin fingers tested the puffy red patch on the bony forehead.

'It was fifty-fifty.' He saw the parsnip face crease into another grin as the man offered his hand.

'Norman Ashe is the name. And yours?'

'Luke Knight,' accepting the handclasp.

'I shan't forget.'

'Me neither.'

10

THE workshop was buzzing. Women ablaze with indignation clustered round Bella, staring at the black sticky mess coating the tools in her drawer.

'What's happened?' Phyl asked, shouldering in for a better look.

Bella pointed to a knothole in the bench top. 'Some joker's poured oil in through there.'

'Joker? Ain't no joke, it's a filthy trick.'

Resentment flared up in a barrage of words.

'Victimization, that's what it is . . .'

'Same trouble we had before all over again . . .'

'Them bloody men wants a dose of their own medicine . . .'

'Real mean I calls it, picking on her. She's got troubles enough . . .'

Bella heard and stiffened in alarm. How did Gertie know? How could she know? The bubble of fear was pricked and collapsed almost as quickly as it came when she realized it was not Luke they were talking about, but her own dark skin.

Emily, next to her, put an arm round her dejected shoulders and gave her a squeeze. 'Don't let it get yo down, love.'

'Sympathy ain't much cop,' Phyl said. 'We wants action. Where's that ruddy foreman? He shouldn't be allowed to slide over this lot.'

'I wasn't meaning to stand by with a plate of words and not much else.' Emily came back at her, surprising Bella out of her gloom by such unusual sharpness. 'Edna's already gone to look for him.'

Edna was the charge hand. A short stringy woman who

reminded Bella of an inquisitive rabbit, with her buck teeth and habit of twitching her nose as she talked.

'P'raps we'd better get back to our work then?' Gertie said anxiously. 'Else he'll chase us for slacking – you know what he's like.'

Phyl's long bony face turned to her with an expression of scorn. 'Oh shut up, Gertie! Yer nothink but panic.'

'If Bella agrees, I votes we should all go,' Emily said.

Doris took the opportunity to air her education. 'A deputation to confront him with the *fait accompli.*'

Bella felt Emily's arm tighten and saw a subtle change in her face, as if a leaf of memory had been turned before she said brusquely:

'If yo means show him what'd been done . . . yes.'

A sense of affection for her and for them all filled Bella, but the cloud of depression that had pursued her ever since Luke had walked off into the night didn't budge. Compared with that worry, this piece of nastiness was a pinprick. She was sick with anxiety for him; the conviction that he was in trouble lay like lead in her mind. No word from him. Not a hint of news, but she *knew* as she always did. She had woken in the night with a terrible pain in her stomach and an inescapable nightmarish sensation of disaster. The pain had faded but the fear had stayed. It was with her now, excluding everything else.

'What d'you say, Bel?'

Emily's warm eyes looking at her. Emily's strong arm still across her shoulders. She was surrounded by friendly inquiring faces, all waiting for the word from her that would set them marching on her behalf. To reject their offers of help would be like a slap in the face. They were giving richly of themselves to support her. She ought to be brimming with gratitude and pleasure when all she wanted was to be left alone to battle with the awful growing fear for Luke.

But they were waiting. She must say something. 'All right. If you thinks it'll do any good.' How grudging she sounded!

They marched the length of the workshop, the remarks of the men drowned in whirring machine noise, but well aware of the grins, winks and frowns.

Bella put her head close to Emily's. 'Can't see him.'

'No.'

'What'll we do?'

At the door they came to an indecisive halt, looking back across the shop floor. Not all the men were enjoying their discomfiture, but there were enough to keep resentment on the boil, and Bella felt a stirring of pride. She'd show them she wasn't going to take it meekly.

'He might've gone to the lav,' Emily suggested.

'Then we'll have to wait till he comes back.' Bella was mule-stubborn as indignation began to take hold, though even now it wasn't easy putting up with being the centre of all the interest.

The wait was mercifully short as the door opened and Edna came in. 'Just our flamin' luck. He's off sick. Got the flu so Gawd knows when he'll be back.'

'Who's his deputy?' Phyl asked.

'Cyril Dickson.' The lift of Edna's shoulders said all she felt about him. 'You'll have to clean up as well as you can, Bella dearie. We'll help you, won't we girls?'

There were murmurs of agreement, but the protest had died like a damp squib. Bella felt it in her bones and said as much later when they were eating their sandwiches in the canteen.

'No good giving up. We'll just have to bide our time,' Emily told her. 'He'll be back and we'll tell him then.'

'There really oughter be a way of putting a stop to it ourselves,' Bella said, without much heart.

'You mean like sabotage their infernal machines?' Doris was giggling.

'No I don't.'

'Well what then? An eye for an eye, I say.'

'Poor lamb, it's a crying shame. She's enough to put up with every day of her life without this.'

Gertie again ... fat old bag! With nerves already on edge, Bella couldn't take this soapy sympathy, or the sideways hint that she wasn't like the rest.

'Oh stuff it!' she snapped. 'I hates it when folk makes mountains out of nothink.'

Gertie reddened and opened her mouth as if to say something more, but didn't, which increased Bella's annoyance. Her earlier feeling of warmth towards her workmates was in danger of melting away. She said:

'I bet I knows who did do it.'

'And I know too. It's old Hedgehog isn't it?' Doris leaned across the table, seeking Bella's eyes, eager with suggestions. 'We could lift his tools and slot them in other racks, or lose them altogether. Serve him right.'

'That's supposing he was the beggar as did it,' Phyl said coolly. She found Doris difficult to take.

'Course he did it.' Doris was firm. 'Written all over him. Plain as the nose on your face ... plainer if that's possible.' The dislike was mutual.

Emily had finished her last sandwich and was folding the paper bag, slipping it into her attaché case. 'I knows what *is* plain. Bella's right, we should help ourselves.'

'Take turns as watchdog ... don't make me laugh.' Doris licked her fingers and smiled scornfully.

Emily ignored her. 'We should make a formal complaint using the proper channels. The foreman ain't here and Cyril Dickson's worse'n useless, which leaves Mr Heliwell.'

She might have suggested God by their stunned reaction. Even Bella was jerked out of her preoccupation, thinking – Emmie's got the knack all right; she can make people sit up and take notice – trying to imagine any of them having the nerve to approach the factory manager with a complaint. His frosty manner and piercing gaze could reduce even the boldest to the size of a pea, almost without a word having been spoken. Would Emmie really have enough courage?

'You wouldn't dare!' Gertie was nervously rolling a button of bread between thumb and forefinger. 'Not go to him *personally*?'

'I'd sweat a bit,' Emily admitted. 'But nothing's easy and besides, I can't stand to see folk getting away with such spiteful capers.'

An awed pool of silence opened round them, into which the crash of crockery being washed and stacked, the scrape of bench legs, the hum of conversation, coughing and laughter fell like stones, the ripples spreading out with hardly any effect.

Phyl, leaning on her sharp elbows, regarded Emily for a long time. When she finally spoke her voice was hard. 'If we're going to complain about rights, then there's somethink else just as pressing.'

'Wages?' It was a statement rather than a question and Bella thought that she and Emmie had talked about this before.

Phyl nodded. 'I don't see why we get less than the men when we works just as hard and as long. How can anybody live on twenty-six bob a week? Bread's just gone up again, and meat ... dunno when I last tasted it.'

'Yo knows the old argument.'

'Families to support? That ain't no argument, that's a good solid reason.'

Everyone knew what she meant. Her husband had been killed at Mons early on in the war, leaving her with three little kids.

'Dilution of women in the factories they call it don't they?' Doris giggled again. 'Sounds like washing up water.'

'Shut yer mouth,' Phyl said. 'Well, Emmie?'

Emily took a little while before saying: 'I dunno. Needs some thinking out.'

Bella was impressed by the fact that Emily hadn't backed out straight away. She wanted to ask her what there was to think out, but the buzzer interrupted, and all she said was: 'It 'ud take some guts to handle him.'

They were at the canteen door when Emily said to her: 'I

think I could find the guts if I had to, but there's no point in asking for more wages if yo can't back it up.'

'What's that supposed to mean?'

'Making sure everyone's behind yo a hundred per cent. So as yo can say – No rise, no work – and mean it.'

Bella was alarmed. There had been a strike at the docks before the war when the Admiral had been a docker. She could remember the hardship, the bitterness, the fights.

Emily looked at her shrewdly. 'Not so easy is it? Anyone can blow off steam, but doing something's a different kettle of fish.'

They walked on in silence for a moment. Problems were spiking up all round. She must have looked worried because Emily asked:

'Had any news?'

Bella had already confided the story of the night excursion to Old Ford Road and the question brought it all back. She tried to cover up with flippancy. 'Not a whisper ... not even a squeak!'

'They say no news is good news,' Emily said.

'In this case?'

'Yo're right. What a daft remark!'

They looked at one another and laughed a little unsteadily, knowing the anxieties each was carrying.

'Have yo been back to Sylvia's place?' Emily asked.

'Yes. I spoke to her an' all. She's a good sort ain't she? Not a bit stuck up like some of the do-gooders.'

'She cares, that's why. Did she know anything?'

'Only that Luke had been taken as far as Stratford. He was to've stayed with a Mr Graham, but he's been arrested for harbouring deserters and conchies.' All the sick worries coiled up and sprang out in a rush of words: 'Oh Emmie, supposing he was with that Mr Graham. Sylvia said there were two men taken away but she didn't know the name of the other bloke.'

Emily put a soothing hand on her shoulder. 'Yo're only guessing. Yo don't know it was him. Ask, that's what yo must do. Try the N-CF office. If he's been arrested they'll know. They've got lists and lists of just about everyone who is an Objector,' and as Bella hesitated: 'Look, I'll come with yo if yo likes. We could go after work sometime. It's a bit of a way – off Fleet Street – but it's better than fretting over what yo don't know.'

The offer touched Bella deeply. It wasn't only Sylvia who was a good sort – Emmie was gold. She said: 'If you would I'd be that grateful.'

'Of course I will.' Emily hesitated. 'There's something else I wanted to ask. About our Vic.' She eyed Bella as if trying to gauge her reaction before putting the question.

Bella started to blush and the more she told herself not to be a fool there was nothing to blush about, the hotter she got. For once she was glad of her protective brown.

'Last letter he asked me to ask yo if yo'd write to him,' Emily went on. 'Bit of a cheek when he scarcely knows yo, but he gets pretty low in the trenches and letters are a link with home. Course the family writes, but a letter from yo would buck him up no end. He's taken a real fancy to yo.' She hesitated, then with a kind of tenderness, and very quickly as if to make sure of saying everything before she lost the nerve, added: 'Proper smitten he is. Yo don't know how glad I am that he's beginning to take an interest again. Since his girl died a while ago, he's not cared what happened to him.'

Bella's burning blush was followed by a hint of cooler apprehension. They had only met twice, so how could he be smitten? She was attracted to him – she was quite prepared to admit that – but only in a fleeting way. There had been no time for anything else. But she did admire him – tremendously. He was so brave. She said cautiously: 'If it'll help I'll write.' After all, France was a long way off and a lot could happen before they came face to face again . . . if they ever did.

'Thanks!' Emily's expression was full of open gratitude, and Bella had the sudden feeling they were now firmly tied together in common concern for Vic. The feeling deepened and left her slightly shaken. It was stepping into the unkown; something she'd always avoided, but this time *wanted* to do. She smiled rather tremulously.

'I'll get me leg pulled at home . . . writing to a strange soldier!'

'Will they mind?' Emily was anxious.

'Who's left to mind?' The despair for Luke came back like a pea-souper fog, enveloping her. 'The Admiral's asleep half his time nowadays and when he's awake he's not properly present. Goes on about the Duke of Wellington and the Frenchies coming to invade. If it wasn't for Lily I'd go round the twist. "Got his mind in a pleat today," she says and we have a bit of a giggle. She keeps me sane does Lily.' She felt slightly ashamed of scoffing and added quickly: 'It's the change in him that upsets me. I don't mean to make fun of him. He used to be so strong and nothink ever got him down. A good boxer he was. No one ever dared give him any lip.'

Emily looked at her, smiling and interested. 'He sounds a real character.'

'There's another side to him,' Bella went on, surprised at how easy it was to talk to her. 'He ain't all brawn. Rare old story-teller too. Course his favourites are always about the old days when he lived in Bristol with his Gran and this old bird called Miss Jarman who used to scare the living daylights out of him as a little kid, because she had a moustache as good as any man and these funny pale eyes that looked straight through you and out the other side. Heart of gold though, he says. She gave his Gran a home when Midnight went off and left her. Midnight's me great-great-grandad that was a slave.' She glanced sideways at Emily to see how she was reacting.

'What happened to him?' Emily asked eagerly, slowing down as they came out into the yard and the chilly February air.

'Worked his passage back to Africa after he was freed. The Admiral says he never knew he'd left a son behind, but I can't believe that. Anyway there was a son – the Admiral's dad – called Jarman after the old bird. He became a sailor and met this slave girl when he went ashore in Montserrat, that's in the West

Indies. He helped her escape from a sugar plantation and brought her all the way back to Bristol and married her. I think that's ever so romantic.' She sighed, adding: 'That's why the Admiral's blacker than the rest of us. He's three-quarters African. My Gran and my Ma were white ... oh listen to me rattling on! I'm getting as bad as him for yarning.' She was astonished at herself. Vic had been right – Emily had a way of getting you to tell her everything.

'Lily sounds a good sort.' Emily had her hand on the workshop doorknob, but she didn't open it.

'Salt of the earth. A proper card. You'd die laughing if you heard some of the stories she tells about being in the chorus touring the Halls. You'd never think to look at her now that she used to kick to her shoulder and do the splits, but she did. Taught me an' all when I was a kid. I still practise because I fancy being a dancer one day. You have to have some dreams don't you, or life 'ud be that drab.'

Emily was smiling broadly and Bella wondered if she'd said too much and made a fool of herself.

'Yo're full of surprises. I'd like to meet Lily ... I'd like to meet them all.'

Warm with relief and pleasure, and astounded at all she had let slip to this person who was so friendly, but whom she had known such a very short time, Bella said: 'I'd like that too – when there's a chance. But come on or we'll be late.'

They went into the workshop, Bella not sure whether she was coming or going; relieved to get back to her bench and the workshop hubbub which wrapped protectively round her. As she worked her mind kept hopping between Emily, Vic and Luke, gradually centring more and more on Luke. Emily was wise. It was much better to find out the truth. At least she was free from making the supper now that Lily had come to live in Golden Street, and she could travel to Fleet Street without worrying.

But the day and the astonishments were not over. As she was packing up at the end of the shift, old Hedgehog left his lathe and advanced towards her. She didn't do anything to show that she had seen him, but couldn't help tension creeping in, which made her clumsy as she put away her tools. Whatever did he want? Why couldn't he leave her alone?

With an oily hand he rubbed his mouth as if to lubricate his speaking. 'Yer a good worker,' he said at last.

If he had told her she had gone white overnight, she couldn't have been more astounded.

He sniffed. 'I've watched y'working. You've a tidy way with yer hands, quick and sure.'

She couldn't speak for astonishment and stared at him, wondering suspiciously if he was making fun of her.

He squeezed his eyes together twice as though he was having difficulty in finding words. 'As good as any apprentice lad and I've seen a good few of them.'

Bella remained speechless, unable even to say, 'Thank you'.

He nodded and sniffed again. 'I'd never've thought a woman could do it – a blackie an' all, but I've seen it and it's true. You keep going gel ... keep going.' He looked steadily at her for a moment then, with a final encouraging nod, stumped out of the workshop.

Utterly confused, Bella exchanged looks with Emily who had come to join her. 'What about that then?'

'Shows people ain't always what they seems. Yo can't judge by first impressions – I found that out a long time ago.'

Bella put the last tool into the bench drawer and closed it. 'I ain't never been so surprised – not even when you said about yer Vic wanting me to write to him.'

Emily smiled and slipped her hand through Bella's arm. 'I'm really pleased about that. Are yo ready for off now?'

They went to the door and out into the greater privacy of the yard.

'I *will* write,' Bella said.

Emily gave her a quick kiss. 'And I *will* come with yo to the N-CF office. Now if yo likes.'

The idea of immediate action – any action, was such a relief that much of the tension in Bella released like a compressed spring. Briefly she thought of the Admiral and Lily. They would worry if she was late, but it couldn't be helped. She smiled at Emily; loving her.

'Yer a real mate,' she said, and together they went to collect their coats.

11

STANDING on the pavement with Emily beside her, Bella looked up at the building that was like and yet so unlike any other in London. Unlike, because it housed the press office of the No-Conscription Fellowship. The clamour of Fleet Street lay behind them but not the air – odours of horse dung and the taint of petrol clung to the sulphur of gradually thickening fog. Now she was here the reality of it was overwhelmingly different from what she had imagined. She felt increasingly uncertain and apprehensive. The policeman with the bushy moustache, quietly waiting near the door, made her anxious. His eyes were almost hidden under the peak of his helmet, but she knew he was looking their way. The temptation to back off and run was great, but that would be cowardly. And besides, she had to find out about Luke. To bolt now would be plain daft. Emily seemed to have no such fears and was marching towards the door. Inwardly quaking, Bella followed, wondering whether the policeman would prevent them from entering. But it didn't happen and they reached the office unchallenged. She began to breathe more easily. Perhaps everything would be straightforward. They would make their inquiries. Find out. Come away. Be safe.

The door to the office was wide open, framing a picture of chaos. Three blue-uniformed men were methodically taking the room apart. Emily and Bella halted and glanced quickly at each other, then without a word turned to go back the way they had come.

It wasn't to be that easy.

'Ah . . . two more birds into the net. Come in . . . come in!' A voice called to them. A complaisant voice.

Trapped, they went reluctantly into the room, and Bella's first impression was of paper being everywhere – in heaps; slithering from desk to floor; crumpled in balls; fanning out from a number of half-open files. She saw a thin pile of *Tribunal* newspapers as well, one of them torn, her gaze going on to the books carelessly dumped on a chair, and in the same sweep took in a group of women standing against one wall. They seemed neither cowed nor defiant. One of them, a cadaverous old-young woman with white hair and pince-nez on a beaky nose, was eyeing her with some curiosity.

They stood for several minutes, deliberately ignored, while the sergeant who had called them back busied himself with a sheaf of paper on the desk at which he was sitting.

Old trout – Bella thought – he's doing it to make us sweat. She sweated. What would they say when he did start his questions? What *could* they say without betraying Luke?

The sergeant looked up with mournful bloodhound eyes, their melancholy emphasized by a great drooping moustache that was neither grey nor ginger but a mixture of both. A face that didn't match the fat self-satisfied voice.

'Well, miss,' he said to Emily. 'You and your friend come to collect, or are you messengers?'

Again Bella was attacked by a strong feeling of apprehension. Emily's face was redder than usual, but she showed no other sign of being ruffled, and took her time over the question.

The man at the desk was getting impatient. He said: 'Well?' again and frowned.

Emily took a little more time before answering: 'Come for my wages.'

Bella looked at her. Had she gone barmy? Wages? It was Friday for sure, but *wages*!

'I do a bit of cleaning here,' Emily went on briskly.

'And what's your name?'

'Emma Prout.'

The confident way she brought out the ridiculous name took

Bella's breath and she was conscious of panic and laughter mixing inside. Her turn next. Whatever would she say?

'Your name, miss?'

'Betsy Napper.' The name came out of nowhere.

The sergeant had made a neat structure with his spread fingertips and was studying it carefully. 'You work here too?'

'Oh ... no!' Bella wasn't sure if that was the right thing to say. Everything was happening too quickly.

'Then why are you here?'

'I ... I'm with me friend. Just for company.'

'I see.'

Another pause, worse than the first. They seemed to be sinking into a pit of mud which grew stickier with every passing minute.

'Well Miss Emma Prout,' he made a meal of the name, 'as you work here you'll know the editor. Care to tell me who it is?'

'Editor?'

'Yes, the editor. Come now, don't waste any more time.'

That had torn it! Emily must be properly foxed. Bella watched as the shorter of the two standing constables picked up a book from the pile on the chair and began to flip through the pages; her own mind blank and incapable.

'Joan Beauchamp, Sergeant. We've already told you several times.'

Bella was shaken out of her daze. Not Emily's voice. The woman with the pince-nez was speaking. She sounded almost yawning with boredom, not scared at all.

The sergeant rapped out: 'She can speak for herself. She's got a tongue.' He glared at them. 'Go and stand over there the pair of you.'

He's narked – Bella thought – good for whoever you are! Her confidence edged up enough to say: 'Why should we? We ain't done nothink. Can't we go?'

The answer came like lightning:

'No you can't. Over there!'

This time neither argued, but joined the group against the wall. The woman in the pince-nez smiled and became a different person – almost impish as she whispered: 'We'll back you.'

They returned the smile, not daring to reply, and the search went on. For precisely what, Bella couldn't begin to imagine; watching drawers being opened and rifled, papers leafed through and abandoned or put aside. The bobby with the book seemed absorbed. She saw him take it to the sergeant and heard the mutter of conversation, but couldn't make out the words.

The sergeant got up. 'That's it for this time.' He sniffed. 'I'm confiscating that lot,' pointing to a pile of paper on the front of the desk. 'And this,' he held up the book.

'I suppose it's too much to hope that when you've finished going through it we'll get any of it back?'

Bella turned so she could see the girl who had asked the question. A pleasant round fresh face, disarmingly innocent.

'Couldn't say I'm sure, Lydia.' The bloodhound eyes creased up and the moustache quivered. 'Can't think how a nice girl like you let yourself get muddled with this nonsense. Not a very happy situation for your parents.' He adjusted his helmet and signalled to one of the constables to collect the files.

Bella felt relief as the door closed behind them and the clatter of boots faded away. An indignant babble of conversation broke out.

'Blessed nerve . . . as if he knew me from the cradle!'

'Thank your lucky stars he didn't confiscate you as well as the files!'

'We were lucky this time. But look at the place . . . just look!'

The woman in pince-nez stared severely at Emily who was picking up paper. 'You've got a nerve. Almost as much as his. Different though.'

Emily blushed furiously. 'I know and I'm ever so sorry. Dunno what came over me. Stress of the moment I suppose.' She gave one of her lop-sided grins, and Bella felt intense laughter inside rising.

'Don't apologize. I admire the way you slid out of trouble. By the way, my name's Catherine Ashe.' The transforming smile was back again and she held out her hand which Emily took after a small hesitation. 'I say, are you really called Emma Prout?'

Emily was crimson. 'No, and she ain't Betsy Napper neither.'

The giggles Bella had managed to suppress, burst out. Everyone was watching, but she just couldn't hold them down any longer.

Emily said: 'It ain't that funny.'

'I knows ...' the hiccups of laughter interrupted and she tried again: 'Really ... we've come about me brother ... Luke ... Lucas Knight.' Why couldn't she stop laughing? There was nothing funny, but the giggles were irrepressible.

'Lucas Knight? Yes I know about him,' Catherine said, extinguishing Bella's laughter. 'We got information yesterday. He is to go before a Tribunal in Stratford on Monday. Is that what you wanted to know?'

The world was reeling. Whatever a Tribunal was, it must mean Luke had been nabbed. Her head buzzed and she felt ill, but fought against being sick. She had come to find out everything.

'Where is he now?' That's not my voice, croaky like Ma Liggins when she's had a few – she thought.

'At the police station in Stratford. I say are you all right?'

'Sit down.' The girl called Lydia pushed a chair behind her knees, and Emily put a hand under her elbow.

Bella remained stubbornly standing. 'I'm fine. What happened? D'you know any more? And what's a Tribunal?' Without realizing, her glance slid to the newspaper.

Catherine Ashe understood. 'Our *Tribunal* is a trifle more feet on the ground than the court your brother will go before.' There was a caustic edge to her voice and she looked very stern, but added with unexpected sympathy: 'I know how you must be feeling. I've a nephew in the same trouble. He's had one hearing and is due for a second. I found out about Lucas because he's at the same police station as Norman.'

'Have you seen him? How is he? What happened?' Bella felt she would choke with questions.

Catherine shook her head. 'I know very little, though I did inquire when I learned he was a CO.' She shrugged. 'They weren't exactly helpful at the station. I didn't even get to see Norman.'

'But didn't they say *anythink*?'

'No more than I've told you . . . and that he's due in court on Monday.'

'They didn't say how he was caught or where they found him?' All eyes were on her and everyone was listening, but she didn't care any more.

The hard expression on Catherine's face melted into something akin to tenderness. 'I only know the bare bones.'

Bella retrieved a sheet of paper she had accidentally pushed off the desk, and tried to deal with the shock of Luke's capture. She hardly knew how she felt and dared not contemplate what was to come.

'Can yo tell us the details? Dó they let relatives and friends into the hearing? We'd like to know please, and the times and where exactly it will be, so as we can go.'

Kind dependable Emily, who was always so practical. Bella felt heartened and full of warm gratitude.

'I'll take you myself,' Catherine said. 'I've got a pass book which entitles me to attend. If you come with me I'll do my best to see you slip in too.'

Bella said deliberately: 'I ain't exactly the type to slip in unnoticed. I wish to Gawd I was.'

For a second Catherine seemed taken aback, then she said: 'If you mean you're brown and I'm white, that doesn't matter one jot. It's the pass book that counts. We may have to argue.'

'She'll do that,' Emily said with conviction. 'Better than me. Words were never my strong point.'

Bella stared in disbelief, but didn't have time to dwell on this surprising opinion because the door opened and the short young policeman came back in. He cleared his throat as he scanned the women and held out the book he was carrying.

On Liberty – Bella read, recognizing it as the one he had been thumbing through.

'This Mr Mill,' he said. 'Where can he be contacted?'

There was an electric pause, then snuffles of suppressed laughter.

'You may have trouble locating him,' Catherine said with barely controlled seriousness.

'Why's that?' A faint pink flush was colouring his pale skin.

But for some reason Catherine couldn't answer and turned away, shoulders shaking. Someone else carried on:

'The gentleman is now resident in either heaven or hell.'

The constable's face was a glory of scarlet as he turned without a word, leaving the room full of laughter.

12

'OUR Lord commands us not to kill,' said the little man in the shabby brown suit and tie thin as a bootlace. 'I believe He is the Highest Authority, so therefore I cannot join any organization for the purpose of killing other people.'

Behind the solid oak table in the panelled room where the Tribunal was being held, four men and one woman were seated. Blotchy colour rose up the chins and face of the white-haired clean-shaven man who seemed to be in charge. The stout body leaned over the table, words spitting out like bullets.

'So you mean to stand there and admit that if a German soldier was about to shoot your mother or your wife, or if . . . pardon me, madam,' he turned with an apologetic nod to the sour-faced woman, 'if he tried to rape them – you, sir, would stand by and let it happen?'

The little man's pallor increased. 'I didn't say that. I'd do my utmost to protect them. Put myself in the way of any bullet. But our Lord said: "Thou shalt not kill". I must obey Him.'

'Poppycock!' The bunched fist slammed down on the table. 'You're a coward, sir. A coward and a cad. Twisting God's words to protect your own miserable shrinking skin. That's all it is.' The outburst seemed to exhaust him and he paused to take a sip of water from the carafe standing on the table, then shuffled some sheets of paper with fidgety fingers, frowning. The action didn't tally with his bombastic words.

The parson, on the chairman's left, cleared his throat, peering with tortoise eyes over the top of steel-rimmed spectacles at the small trembling figure. '"I come not to bring peace but a sword". Our Lord's words again, my good man. What answer have you now?'

'Excellent point, Mr Blenkinsop. Couldn't have put it better myself.' The white head turned, frown gone. 'Get yourself out of that knot if you can.'

'"Love your enemies. Bless them that hate you",' the little man countered hoarsely, bringing out a large white handkerchief from his pocket and wiping his face.

'This is absurd,' said the man in charge. 'We can't spend the day swapping texts. What we have to do is decide on the merit, or lack of it, of the argument and I must say this . . . this person's reasons seem very poor . . . very poor indeed.'

'But how do we decide, Mr Chairman? I mean, his texts were just as much part of the Bible as Mr Blenkinsop's. Sorry to say it I'm sure, but truth . . . well . . . truth's truth.' The man putting the objection sat at the end of the table. His sharp mole features twitched as he spoke and his long thin hands wound together in an agony of nervousness.

'That seems nonsense to me, Mr Copthorne.' The chairman was frowning again, obviously put out.

'I wouldn't go so far as to say nonsense,' said Mr Blenkinsop in his dry way. 'Merely less well informed. A little more attention to the context of the quotations offered would be more in keeping. Study is worth a thousand guesses.'

The chairman arranged his papers in a neat pile and laid two pencils on top in the shape of a T, muttering: 'Yes . . . well . . .' leaving the sentence to trail away.

'What . . .' Mr Copthorne coughed nervously. 'What would the applicant say if we were to offer him the chance of joining the Non-Combatant Corps? After all he does seem a very religious man. Very sincerely religious.'

'Mr Blenkinsop is a very sincerely religious man, Mr Copthorne, but he doesn't shirk his duties.'

Mr Copthorne's hands found and hung on to his lapels as if to keep himself from drowning. 'Er . . . yes . . . of course, but . . . if we were just to ask?'

The chairman was visibly disconcerted. He seemed uncertain whether or not to let the question through, but in the end allowed it with a testy nod of his head. 'The Non-Combatant Corps, er ... whatsy'name?'

'Tomkins, sir,' said the little man, looking ready to cry. 'I should have to refuse if you were to offer me that way out. I see it as no more than a means of releasing another man to fight. I can have no part in that.'

The chairman said: 'Oh one of those Absolutist chappies. I might have known.' His scorn was rasping, and he treated the shrinking Mr Copthorne to an I-told-you-so glance before saying: 'I'm sure we are all agreed on our decision now? Yes. Objection overruled. Next applicant,' checking down a list before him.

The little man was taken out and Lucas ushered in. He stood there feeling his legs shaking uncontrollably, but determined not to give them the pleasure of knowing how scared he was. He straightened his shoulders.

'Name?'

'Lucas Knight.'

The chairman looked up having realigned his pencils and said involuntarily: 'Good Lord!'

All eyes focused on Lucas.

'And where d'*you* come from?'

The words 'Up country from Calabar on the West Coast of Africa' were on the tip of Lucas's tongue. Courage slipping, he said: 'Poplar.'

The frown returned. 'Then why are you here? Wrong district. Must be some mistake.'

'He was apprehended in Copton Street, sir. In the Feathers Public House. Police Constable Weaver arrested him as a deserter, sir,' said the constable who had brought Lucas into the courtroom.

'Deserter? We don't deal with deserters. Case for Army Court Martial. Send him back to his regiment.'

The constable stared stonily into the distance. Lucas got the impression he was holding on to his patience with difficulty. 'Sir, he has received the enlistment form W3236, but failed to comply with the instructions. A technical deserter, sir. Never actually been in camp. Says he wishes to apply for exemption for reasons of conscience. sir.'

'Then why the blazes didn't he do so in the first place instead of wandering out of his area and causing trouble? Thorough-going rogue. Good stretch of Army life'll make a man of him. No business here. A scrounger if ever I saw one. How old are you?'

The direct question made Lucas start. With some difficulty he got out: 'Eighteen.'

'Much too young to have settled opinions. All the same these youngsters, changing their minds every two minutes. Hmm!' He picked up a pencil, made a small circle on the paper before him and scored it through. 'I really don't see why we are supposed to deal with a case of this sort. We have enough problems as it is.' He sounded peevish.

'We ought in all fairness to let the fellow state his case, Mr Chairman.' The Rev. Blenkinsop fingered his dog-collar. 'He is here inescapably. Justice must be seen to be done. You do agree?'

Port-wine red, the chairman scooped up his papers, tapped them together, laid them in an even neater pile and finally agreed. 'Very well, very well.' He glared at Lucas. 'Speak up then. Religious objections?'

'No.'

'No *sir*!'

'No sir,' Lucas croaked, his jaw suddenly cramped and rigid from the nightmare absurdity of what was happening.

'Get on with it, we haven't all day! Explain yourself.'

Lucas wetted his lips with the tip of his tongue. 'It's like this see ...' His voice was no more than a whisper.

'Don't mumble in your boots!'

'LIKE THIS,' Lucas said, bold now as resentment hit him, but scaring himself by the booming of his own voice. 'We gets born by no choosing; no wishing to be. But now we *are* born the life we've got is a kind of treasure. The way I sees it, nobody's got the right to take away this treasure from another person, even if he is a Hun. After all we're all people. What's the point in slaughtering each other?' He looked along the row of tight well-fed faces, hoping for something ... anything that might show a hint of understanding or fellow-feeling. The stone-wall eyes stared flintily back. He went on doggedly: 'Don't you see? Life ain't somethink to be treated like an old paper bag, screwed up and chucked into the gutter without a second thought. It's a ... a diamond. A precious thing we should care for and respect.' Oh Gawd, they thought he was crackers. Row of suet dumplings. Useless, useless – but he must go on though it would be an agony. Go on, go on! Before the chance was lost forever and he was left to kick himself from now till doomsday.

'Totally irrelevant!' The chairman intervened. 'No point in listening to any more. If you can't produce a better reason than this garbled nonsense then your case is closed.'

'But I haven't finished,' Lucas said desperately. 'You must hear it all. Justice must be seen to be done. *He* said that,' pointing at the clergyman.

'Impudent puppy ...' the chairman began, but didn't continue, leaving a small wordless space which Lucas seized before he could be interrupted again.

'If you looks ... really looks I mean, not like most people who go around with their eyes shut ... if you really looks at the world, there's so much beauty – and a lot of ugliness I grant you – but the beauty's there and that's the important thing. I reckon that's what it's all about. Beauty. Looking at it and trying to make it in whatever way is right for you. The war ain't any kind of beauty. It's ugly and wasteful. What right have I, or you – anybody, to go round killing and killing. There ain't no worse sin and I can't ... *won't* take part.' He looked at the floor wishing Bella was there to hear. Perhaps she might then have understood. 'That's all I have to say.'

His words seemed suspended in the air for seconds after he had finished speaking. A strange confusing silence reigned as if his cheek in being there, let alone in concocting such a statement, had temporarily taken the wind out of their sails. It was the woman who recovered first. She craned her long neck towards him.

'Tell me, young man, do you eat cheese?'

Lucas stared, baffled. 'Yes, ma'm.'

'Then I put it to you that you are showing every sign of being a hypocrite. To eat cheese means you take part in the killing of those maggots whose job it is to provide you with the cheese. You cannot accept one kind of killing and reject another.'

The logic and truth of this was quite beyond him, but the petty stupidity was not. He felt outraged. 'I was speaking of human life, ma'm. Maggots make a meal of us all soon enough. I ain't going to provide 'em with extra rations just at present.'

The chairman rose to his feet, spluttering. Through the turmoil in his mind Lucas caught the words, 'Heard enough ... not even British ...' and the final judgement, 'Objection overruled.'

He reached the passage outside the courtroom door before the reality of those words hit him, and the door into the street before he remembered what Norman Ashe had told him.

'Here, I want to appeal. I've the right,' he demanded.

'Don't make me laugh, sonny,' said the same policeman who had been with him all morning. 'You forfeited yer rights when you let yerself get nabbed. Fancy going into a pub!' He put a hand on Lucas's shoulder in quite a friendly way. 'My best advice to you is play it quiet and don't make no more trouble. That way you'll maybe get through not too bad.'

Behind him, parked at the kerb was an army van with two khaki giants standing by it, and a few feet away ... Bella! A broad red-cheeked girl with her. The sight of her bewildered him. She came pushing through the knot of spectators who had gathered to see the fun and jeer. He could see she was on the point of tears.

'Have they let you go ... no they can't have ... what's happening ... where are they taking you ... I tried to get into the courtroom but they wouldn't let me.'

Lucas hugged her speechlessly, seeing the two military policemen closing in. The moment of parting outside Sylvia Pankhurst's place was nothing to this. He had no idea how she could have found him and his earlier wish vanished because her distress was acute and bit into him. It could only get worse. He wanted to tell her how important she was to him; say sorry for not always paying attention; wish her well. But the words wouldn't come. She smelled sweetly of warmth and home.

'Right y'are, constable. If you've finished with this party we'll take over.' The larger of the two khaki giants loomed over them both.

'Keep yer nose clean and do as yer bid,' the policeman told Lucas.

'Left it a bit late now ain't he? Daft bugger!' The soldier laughed and said to Lucas scornfully: 'Come on, Sambo ... into the van with you,' grasping his arm.

It was an agony to let her go and he felt her trembling. He managed to whisper: 'Nothink to tell ... all me own fault ... take care,' before she stood back, eyes huge and wet in the oval of her face, hands clenched at her sides. As they led him to the van he wondered briefly how the Admiral would take it. He was not much of a grandson to be proud of by the old man's standards.

Inside the van he fell across half-seen knees and feet. He muttered: 'Sorry, mate,' scrambling on to the opposite seat, then thrust his hands between his knees and squeezed them together to stop the shaking, unable to do more then hang on to the fact that, though they had caught him, he was still free in his mind.

'Luke?'

Lucas took a furtive glance across the van. Two men were sitting there. One, a stranger, had his head hunched between his bony shoulders and didn't raise his eyes. The other ... holy Moses!'

'Stan Jeffries!'

His hand was seized in an iron grip and shaken vigorously, and a wide smile of real pleasure lit up the thin grey face he remembered so vividly. Stan said: 'By golly, lad, it's good to see you though I wish it were in better circumstances.'

'They nicked you an' all,' Lucas said, doubly depressed by this fresh twist of fate. 'Thought you'd managed to dodge 'em.'

'So I did for a time. But rooting through dustbins for grub that ain't there, looking over yer shoulder while you does it ... well, there's no future in that. Oh, if you've a bob or two put by and some canny friends willing to risk their necks on your account, then maybe.' He shook Lucas's hand again. 'Friends like you. Shan't forget what you did for me in a hurry. Looking after me for a whole fortnight. Kept me going.'

'Oh that! That weren't nothink.' He didn't want to talk or even think about that distant other world.

Stan released his hand and sat back. 'Counts more than you know. And those talks we had. Got me seeing things in perspective. It was all we said as decided me running is the wrong way of going about things. Bothering about yer own skin and not much else. Stan – I thought – speak out. Tell the truth. Somebody's got to be first ... not that I can claim that glory. Don't get me wrong when I say you've got to *fight* for what you thinks is right.'

An echo from the Admiral! Lucas didn't answer, lapsing back into his former gloom. He wished the van would move. Why didn't it? Anything would be better than this eternal waiting.

'Keep yer pecker up, chum,' Stan said as the doors opened letting in a blast of cold blinding sunlight.

Two figures there – one being shoved inside, the other clambering after him. One of the soldiers was swearing profusely and kicking through the legs. 'Move up y'sniffin' conchie skunks. We're on our way to home sweet home. Can't wait to see our Sarge when he gets his mitts on you bunch o' fairies!'

Lucas blinked, listening to the sound of huge rough palms rubbing together in glee and watching Norman Ashe stumble to the seat beside him. The door slammed and the van started up, moving with a jolt down the street. As it juddered over the cobbles, his failing courage began to drain away entirely; his mind insisting on leaping ahead to all kinds of imagined horrors. I can't take no more today, he thought, and was immediately ashamed. Stan was here and Norman and the other geyser, whoever he was. All of them in the same boat. With a great effort he dragged back from the precipice of what might be, understanding clearly that from now on if he was to survive he must live from moment to moment. It was the only way.

13

IF only she knew!

A week had passed since the Tribunal. A week of wondering what had become of Luke. Seeing the army van drive away down the street had been the worst moment of Bella's life. She tried not to think about it too much, though that was difficult. The picture would keep flashing into her mind at the most unexpected moments making her seethe with fury at the way Luke had been treated. Shoved and pushed and ordered about as if he was dirt. And *Tommies* doing it! Of course it was their job, she knew that, but they didn't have to enjoy it so much. That they had, was another blow of a different kind. She couldn't see them as heroes any more. Luke wasn't a criminal. All he was doing was standing up for what he believed to be right. Oh, what a mess! And he's brought it on himself, she thought, her anger growing and twisting round to aim at Luke this time – brought it on the Admiral ... and me! The picture came again, cutting sharp, so that temporarily she forgot that she and Emily were being taken by the foreman to see the awesome Mr Heliwell; factory manager; God!

'I'd just like to know who went telling tales,' Emily said, bringing Bella back into the present and the anonymous factory passage, along which they were walking. 'But no matter what happens, no one can say yo ain't brave, Bel. You'd've made a splendid Suffragette ... the best sort.'

Bella went hot with embarrassed pleasure while still thunderstruck by the fact that she had stood up in the canteen in the dinner break, amongst all those women, men too, and talked about asking for better wages. It had been almost like taking part in a film. The buzzer had interrupted before they'd taken a proper vote, but that was unimportant. She had done it – though how it had come about, she still wasn't sure. Part of it grew out of an argument with Emily who said the time wasn't right and they needed to go about things more cautiously; part came from her own tense mood which made her ripe for reacting against Doris's silly goading that had got under her skin and finally brought her to her feet. Whatever the reason, it had happened and she was glad. Even now, shaking like a leaf, she was still unrepentant.

The foreman led them into a small reception hall. He seemed genuinely upset. It showed in his walk and now in his words. 'Blowing off steam about yer wages! Why didn't you come to me? Now yer in the cart. *He* don't hold with underhand methods.'

'Who told him?' Bella asked, riled by this injustice. 'Talking ain't underhand . . . we was only talking.'

'How should I know who told him?' He crossed the worn Turkey rug which covered most of the floor and tapped on the manager's door.

A voice called: 'Enter.'

'The ladies you asked to see, sir.'

They went into a large square room that had brown embossed paper halfway up the walls and cream paint above. Two windows with roller blinds looked out into a quiet side street. There was a smell of lavender floor polish and cigarette smoke. Mr Heliwell was sitting behind a heavy oak desk with a leather top and a lot of papers piled in untidy heaps. Not in keeping with the way he dresses, Bella thought, faintly surprised to find this an encouragement, as if she'd spied a crack in his armour. The dragon himself sat very upright behind the semi-chaos, his thin face and hooked nose fringed with neatly trimmed mutton-chop whiskers. He wore a gold-topped stick pin in his tie which was black, and had a black armband round the left sleeve of his good tweed jacket. Bella felt unwilling sympathy for him in whatever loss he had suffered. He waved towards two hard chairs.

'Sit down, sit down.'

It was more than Bella had expected even though his testy manner was not welcoming. They sat edgily, while Mr Heliwell got up, went to the window and stood looking out, hands clasped behind his back. The atmosphere changed noticeably. Bella's sympathy began to wilt and when he said without turning round: 'What's all this about a meeting in the canteen?' in a voice that would have kippered a herring, her heart skipped a beat and her arms weakened.

Neither of them replied, each waiting for the other, and he turned, coming back to the desk and the chair which he spun round in a way that revealed his annoyance.

'Come along ... you've got tongues haven't you?'

'It's like this ...'

'We were only ...' they said together then stopped.

'I'll hear one at a time. You first,' pointing at Bella.

Speaking in the canteen had cost an effort, but it was nothing to this. Mouth and mind went dry simultaneously. All she could think of was that his cupped ears moved as he talked, just like Luke's did. The comparison was unnerving, all the more so because in every other way they were poles apart. This man would support the war to the last drop of blood she was sure. That ought to make her respect him.

'Well?' He had put on spectacles with gold wire rims, and was impatiently tapping a pencil on his blotter.

Bella said nervously: 'We only wanted to see if we were of a mind.'

'About what?'

'Wages.'

'Ah!' he said softly, allowing the silence to develop again then cracking it with a rapid: 'And *were* you of a mind?'

Bella felt trapped. 'I ... I dunno. The buzzer went before we'd time for a proper vote.'

'There was a good show of hands in favour,' Emily said quickly.

He gave her an icicle stare. Emily's colour heightened, but she didn't look away. Impressed and wanting to match her in nerve, Bella said hastily:

'We'll take another vote and if it's in favour then we'll come to you with the findings. We wants to do everything fair and honest, nothink underhand like.' She didn't dare look at him properly and risked only a single swift glance. He was paler than ever, his mouth set and grim. She began to quake in earnest.

'You're a troublemaker, Miss . . . er . . . Miss . . .'

'Knight,' in a croaky whisper which was ignored.

'I don't quite know what you think you are doing or why, but I'll tell you this – there has never been any problem in my works and I don't intend that there should be now. We have a fine war record. Fine. High output. It will stay that way.'

'But it ain't true!' Bella protested, a fierce sense of injustice overcoming her awe. 'I've had me tool drawer messed up with oil and I ain't the only one. Not that I'm complaining now. It's over and done with, but if you thinks everybody is content, then you don't know the half.' She was staggered at herself saying such things and was not really surprised when he snapped:

'That's quite enough. I had hoped to settle this matter in a civilized way, but I see that it is quite out of the question. I shall, however, settle it. You may finish your day's work. Fortunately it is Friday, so you can collect your wages as usual. I shall not expect you to return. I am not a vindictive man, so I shall allow you a Leaving Certificate. As for you,' he looked sternly at Emily. 'If you are prepared to behave yourself and make no more trouble, then you may stay on. That is all.'

It was really no more than she'd expected, but Bella was still stunned, hearing the words of dismissal spoken. The thing that really rankled was her failure to put the case to him in a clear concise way. She'd let down all her mates and was a failure. There was nothing more she could do. With the bravado of hopelessness she added:

'You want to go and talk to some of yer work folk instead of sitting here in yer cosy room. You might learn somethink then.' That was the Leaving Certificate down the drain! She stood up, meaning to go. The interview had been over minutes back. But she had reckoned without Emily.

'If she goes, I go.'

'Emmie . . . no!' Bella was horrified. She had never intended this.

'I mean it, Bel. I should've given in my notice a long time back and joined the VAD. If I've got to be in this ruddy war I'd as soon lend a hand mending folk as help kill them. That's what I call civilized.' She was talking directly to Mr Heliwell now. 'And your notion of what's vindictive and what ain't needs a few layers of dust knocked off.'

Bella felt like cheering, and Mr Heliwell's face underwent a considerable change. A hard winter's frost in his voice, he said:

'I see. There's no point in continuing this unseemly conversation. I've said what I said and it stands. Good day to you.'

There was nothing to do but go. At the door Emily hesitated.

'Well what now?' The frost was thick with ice.

Emily said with difficulty: 'The Leaving Certificate. Will I get one?'

Mr Heliwell fixed her with a gimlet stare. 'People who make their own beds must lie on them. If you wish to leave that is your affair, but don't expect help from me.'

'The lousy old bastard,' Bella said, when they were out of earshot and halfway back to the workshop. 'Oh you were grand, Emmie, really grand. But you didn't oughter have done it. What'll you do now? You won't be able to get a job for six weeks without a certificate.'

'Don't rub it in,' Emily said ruefully. 'I've a bob or two in hand and if the worst comes to the worst I can go back home to Brum and help Mam with her lodgers. What about yo?'

Bella sighed. 'Dunno really. I'll have to find somethink, that's for sure. Can't live on fresh air. I'd like to join that new Women's Army Auxiliary Corps but . . .' But what? But the

Admiral would gripe? But Lily would be upset? Truth in both, but not the real reason which she didn't know how to explain even to herself.

'Why don't yo come with me when me six weeks is up? We could do nursing together.'

'All that blood ... no thanks!' Bella shivered. She looked at Emily with admiration. 'Dunno how you can face that. You'll make a lovely nurse.'

'Oh it won't half be a relief to be out of this place.' Emily sounded joyous.

'Why *did* you stay then?' Bella put the question almost timidly.

Emily considered as they left the passage and went out into the yard. The grey lid of the day was pressing down more heavily with the on-coming of evening and the cold had intensified.

'It was good at first because I was helping make things that was to do with Peter's job. He was a pilot first, before he joined the Kite Balloon unit. Then, when he was ... killed, I just didn't care. I was keeping body and soul together. Then it was a sort of feeling for my workmates. Then yo came.'

'Whatever difference did I make?' Bella couldn't believe she had any bearing at all.

'Hard to pin down really. There was the coincidence of yo being at the station and then turning up here. But it's much more than that. Yo're tough and full of spirit – different from a lot.'

'I knows *that*!'

'I don't mean being brown, yo dafty. That ain't nothing to do with it.' Emily paused, then added: 'Perhaps it does though. When things ain't easy yo either goes under or takes a deep breath and comes up fighting. Yo're the second sort. Cheered me no end yo did one way and another.'

Bella began to giggle.

'What have I said?' Emily looked at her, mystified but beginning to laugh with her.

'Just you saying everythink I've been thinking ... about you,' she tried to quieten the giggles. 'And his *face* when you told him where to get off!' She went into a fresh burst of laughter. 'Oh I won't half have a lot to tell Vic when I writes.'

It was true, she discovered as she settled herself into a comfortable nest in bed that night with pencil, paper and the Bible on her knees for a support. It was always surprisingly easy to write to Vic. Just as it was easy to talk to Emily. She wasn't sure that if they were face to face the ease would remain. But for now there was so much to say. She crooked her knees into a better angle and began to write, telling him everything that had happened that day – the sacking; Emily's plan to become a nurse; the surprising support of the Admiral because he approved of the way she had stood up for herself. She even found herself writing about Luke being a conchie, but tore that up and went back to her own news and the piece of luck:

Lily met an Old Flame the other day (she has lots of Old Flames) and this one runs a Music Hall somewhere down the Elephant and Castle way or did. It has been closed for a bit. I don't know why something to do with not being able to get enough people to do the donkey work I think but he is trying to get it going again for the sake of the Tommies on leave he says. Lily asked me if I would like to have a job there. He had offered it to her but she says I am much more nippy on my feet and she creaks something chronic with her rheumatics nowadays. It would be as a sort of dogsbody doing errands and some sewing in the wardrobe (that is what they call the folk as make the costumes so don't split your sides at the thought of me inside a cupboard!). There might be the chance of a bit part now and again in sketches and things Lily says. Of course my colour is against me as I told her but she says don't be daft and anyway I would do splendid as a dancer and I might work up an Eastern Routine. I have a flair for it she says. I am not so sure about that but it would be a dream come true because I have always fancied being a dancer ever since I was a nipper and I do my exercises regular and a bit of dancing in my own room. It's a lovely chance and just like what I've often dreamed about but for all that I don't know about trying for the job because I really fancies being in the WAAC with the war on and all and I would if the Admiral was not so poorly. His chest has been troubling him these last two weeks. It all started when he got out of bed one night and went into the street with nothing on but his nightshirt and that queer old hat his Grandmother Jess give him. A neighbour knocked us up to say he was marching up and down the street saying he was going to K O any Frenchie as got big ideas about invading our house! Goodness knows how he got out there without me or Lily hearing. The only bit of luck was there was no air raid on at the time though if there had been we would have been up anyway.

Bella glanced at the candle which was almost burnt out. She'd have to look sharp if she was to get this finished ready to post in the morning.

Here is me going on and on about everything as has happened today and it is back to front because I should have started by saying thanks for all the nice things you wrote. You say you like me because I am different. I don't know what you mean really. I know I am different. You can't have a dark skin and live in Poplar all your life and not know that. Anyway I know as you mean it kindly and that makes a nice change. I hope you are keeping well and chirpy. I think about you every night and say a bit of a prayer. Not that I am much of a one for churchgoing but if there is anything in it I would hate to have not made good use of it to help keep you and our Jack and our Luke safe.

I will write again soon.

Your friend

Bella.

PS. I am glad to hear you are learning to play the banjo. Where did you get it?

PPS. Sorry this is in pencil but I am writing in bed.

With a small sputtering sound the candle gave a last flicker and went out. In the darkness Bella felt for the chair and shuffled the writing paper on to it, slithering down into the warmth of her bed. Strange how easy it was to write to Vic – easier than it would be to write to Luke somehow, which didn't seem to make sense.

Luke! The lack of him was suddenly very painful. She shut her eyes tightly, trying to switch off her thoughts, but the ache would not go away and the moon, piercing a worn place in the curtain, cut across her face like a knife. She wriggled and burrowed deep into the bedclothes, but sleep was elusive and for a long time she lay there wondering what was happening to him.

If only she knew. If only she knew!

14

'SQUAD ... Atte – e – en – SHUN! Come on y'dozy lot. Heels together arms to yer bleedin' sides thumbs down the seams of yer trousers head up chin in ... BLOODY 'ELL! Yer like a lot o' tater sacks tied round with flamin' string. We'll start again. Standat ... EASE!'

In the middle of the gritty dusty patch which was the parade ground of Hounslow Barracks, Lucas had remained 'at ease', unmoving. Behind him the three other Objectors were also refusing to obey the drilling orders. The knowledge gave him a certain strength, but even so he didn't dare meet the popping eyes of the sergeant, and stared instead at a bar of cloud drifting in a westerly direction.

''Ere yew. Golliwog!' The sergeant had glared at each of the four in turn, singling out Lucas for particular attention. 'Y'may be a bleedin' cannibal but don't let on y'can't speak English. I knows all about you and yer funny friends. Don't y'go thinking y'can start pulling yer sniffin' tricks round me. If y'knows what's good for yer, y'll listen. Now then this time when I gives you a bloody order you obey it. Understand? That goes for you other buggers an' all. Right. Get it this time or I'll have the lot of yer in the cookhouse spudbashing till they comes out of yer bleedin' ear'oles.' He twitched his shoulders as if making sure they too were correctly positioned. 'SQUAD ... SQUA–A–A–D ... Atten–e–en–SHUN ... that's better that's better. SQUA–A–A–D ... RRI–I–IGHT ... TURN. Oh sniffin' 'ell!'

'You do as he says or I'll smash yer face after,' the soldier on Lucas's left hissed through unmoving lips.

Lucas didn't respond. The part of him that wasn't scared stiff was observing the chaos with amusement. He was sandwiched between two faces, the men either side staring across him at each other. It was obvious that right and left were mysteries to a few of the raw recruits surrounding him and he warmed to them.

'Yew 'orrible little creepy-crawlies you!' the sergeant brayed. 'What have I done to deserve such a bunch of thick'eads! Yer right's what yer writes with and yer left's the one left over when yer writin', if any of y'can, which I doubts. RIGHT. If any of yer forgets this time I'll double yer round this parade ground till yer bleedin' eyes stand out on stalks.' He drew in his breath, swelling his barrel chest and reinforcing his ramrod back. 'AS YOU WERE. Standat ... EASE. SQUAD ... SQUA–A–AD ... ATTE–E–EN–SHUN!'

The four Objectors remained 'at ease'. This time there was no reprieve. With remarkable swiftness the sergeant moved his bulk to within a hand-spread of Lucas, towering over him.

'Whatsyername?'

'Lucas Knight.'

'Sergeant!'

Lucas kept his mouth obstinately closed. He wasn't going to be tricked into kowtowing again. He'd learned his lesson at the Tribunal.

'SERGEANT!' Blue jaw and bulging eyes were thrust close to his face with a powerful odour of pickled onion breath. 'You think yer a comedian do yer, somethink orf the 'Alls? Well Golliwog, this 'ere's not the place for entertainment. This 'ere's the place for marching. MCALISTER! JACKSON!' the bellow was deafening. 'This joker's forgotten how to march, so we're going to show him. You an' all.' He glared over Lucas's head at the other Objectors. 'The man either side of them three conchie bleeders take an arm each. Bring 'em out. Drag 'em if necessary. That's right ... Now then, show 'em any way you fancy, but *show* 'em. By the left ... QUI–I–ICK ... MARCH!'

Lucas's arms were gripped hard. Jackson he knew well enough – an ex-butcher and loudmouth who had already slung several insults in his direction. The other was a gangling raw-boned youth still in civvie suit and cloth cap (because the supply of uniforms had run out) who had trouble in looking after his hands and feet.

'Leftrightleftrightleftright.'

As the commands came, Lucas was pulled forward and forced into a trot. The pace quickened and they reached the corner of the parade ground on the heels of Stan and his tormentors who were kicking at his ankles as they ran. Not to be outdone, Jackson stuck out a foot. Unable to save himself, Lucas tripped and catapulted forwards, landing with an agonizing crash and pulling his other captor on top of him. Loose grit raked his palms and elbows. He lay winded. The pain, excruciating for a moment, stopped him from trying to get up. But he wasn't allowed time to recover. Jackson yanked at his arm before the rawboned lad was on his feet; dragging him from under the bodyweight and a few yards along the ground, shouting out as he went:

'Whatcha do that for, Sambo? Trying to be funny, eh? Trying to hurt old Chalky here? Or were y'trying to scarpa? Know what happens to shirkers as get sniffin' ideas about running off? Shot ... that's ... what ...' each word accompanied by a violent jerk.

'Leave off, Jackers,' Chalky said, on his feet now and dusting himself down. 'It were you as stuck yer ugly great boot out. Whatcha do it for?'

'We don't want no fancy circus acts!' The great voice boomed across the parade ground, chopping off Chalky's complaint. 'Get that bastard moving or I'll have the three of you in the guardroom! Leftrightleftright ... MOVE!'

Jackson started to run, muttering: 'Don't blame me for this conchie bastard's tricks!'

Desperately Lucas tried to scramble up, but before he could, Chalky in a panic had seized his other arm and was racing full tilt diagonally away from Jackson. Crucified between them, pain racking down his arms through his ribs, tearing the full length of his body, there was no way he could get up. All he could do was arch forward, letting his knees take the full brunt of punishment in an attempt to protect his tender groin. When at last the torment was over, he could barely stand. The others were no less shaken and exhaustion clung round them long after they had been taken back inside, persisting through the rest of the day and into the yawning night.

'You awake, Luke?'

'Yes.'

'Thought so.' Stan rolled over to face him, keeping his single blanket tight round his body. There was an icy blast whiffing under the ill-fitting door of the room in which the four of them were locked. To add to their discomfort, there were no pillows or mattresses.

'Can't sleep,' Lucas said. 'It's having the gas burning all the time. And me knees. It's just as if I'd got toothache in 'em.'

Stan got up and came closer. 'Here, let's have a look.'

Gingerly Lucas parted his rough blanket, exposing two puffy lumps of raw bruised skin and bone.

'Gawd, they're a nasty pair of suet pudd'ns. You want to watch them.'

'About all I can do.'

'Bloody butchers!' Stan said with quiet intensity.

'That were Jackson's trade before the army took him.'

'Yer a tough'n, Luke. We'll need plenty of your sort after this lot's over.'

Lucas crooked his legs carefully, involved with trying to ease the pain. 'Who will?'

'Us workers.'

'Oh that!' He didn't feel in the mood for jawing about revolution and the downtrodden workers. He didn't dispute what Stan said, but had a sneaking feeling that most wouldn't thank anybody for telling them so, and he for one wasn't going to try. He'd leave that to the Stans of this world. There was too much else he wanted to do, like staying sane right now.

'The war's taken the blinkers off,' Stan went on and Lucas could see the familiar light of enthusiasm in his eye. 'Nothing can ever be the same again and the important thing is to keep 'em off.'

'Give it a rest,' Lucas said wearily.

'On his soap box again?' Norman asked from somewhere under his blanket. He emerged, blinking.

'Sorry – didn't mean to wake you.' Stan was contrite on both counts, apologizing to Lucas by mocking himself with a rueful expression and pointing at his own head.

'Couldn't sleep.' Norman nodded towards the rumbling roaring heap that was Cyril Bennet. 'Him and the light. It wasn't the talk.' He hotched into a sitting position, back against the wall, huddling in his blanket, hair spiky and upstanding. As if the parsnip had suddenly sprouted – Lucas thought, and grinned.

'What you so happy about?' Stan asked.

'Can't help it . . . look at him!' thumbing at Norman.

'As if someone sat on my face when I was a kid you mean?' Norman said aimiably. 'My brother used to say God was in a bit of a hurry when he made me and put my nose on hot and it ran all over my face. I don't mind being a bit funny looking really, but I sometimes wish I was more handsome – like you chaps.'

'What . . . me handsome?' Stan said. 'You'll make me die laughing.'

'It would be a good way to go,' Norman yawned and stretched.

'Not for me.' Lucas spoke equally lightly, but he didn't like casual jokes about dying. He looked enviously at the snoring Cyril. 'How can he sleep?'

'Lucky he does,' Stan settled himself more comfortably against the wall. 'If he didn't he'd not last after treatment like he got today. He's skin and bone as it is.'

There was a lull, broken only by Cyril's snores changing to coughs in his sleep and the steady hiss of gas. Norman had lain down again, arms crossed behind his head.

'You know what I miss most of all is my bed,' he said

suddenly. 'A thick down mattress that I sink into and lose myself . . . glorious!'

It was the first direct allusion he had made to home life. Lucas knew all about Stan; Stan's wife; Stan's job; Stan's strong socialist opinions. But Norman had skirted round personal things until now, and wanting to know more Lucas said:

'You says that as if you means it.'

'Of course I mean it.'

'Funny sort of thing to say you miss most.'

'I'm naturally lazy.'

Lucas couldn't believe this and suspected he was being fobbed off again, in which case there didn't seem much point in going on asking questions. He wished the ache in his legs would stop.

'Perhaps it's escape really,' Norman added more seriously. '*You* must know what it's like to want to bury your head in the sand sometimes – when problems get too big.' He twisted round so that he could look at Lucas. 'I was thinking when I had the jitters before they dragged us out this morning . . . I was thinking it must be much worse for you – being black. You'd get picked on twice over.'

Lucas did not answer immediately, but observed them looking at him, their expressions alert, expectant, sympathetic. He was tempted not to answer, and wouldn't have bothered if he hadn't liked both of them so much. He smiled at them.

'I don't need no sympathy you know, not yours nor no one's. There's truth in what you says, I ain't denying that. Me skin's a sort of badge. Look at him – he's different . . . that's what white people thinks. And even when they means to be kind, like you just did, it's as if they thinks being black is a sort of illness I ain't got a chance of getting over but would like to if I could. Perhaps they thinks I'd like to be white. They're nuts! Don't suppose you ever thought there ain't nothink wrong with being black, it's only the white people what thinks there is.' He couldn't tell if they understood him. There was a frozen blankness in both faces. 'Y'know somethink? I had this mate at school whose parents were Polish. He was born in Poland but came to the East End when he were still in nappies. He were a good kid, and when he opened his mouth he didn't sound no different from all the other kids. Talked broad Cockney, and nobody ever asked him where he come from like they did me. Didn't make no difference that *my* family's been English for more'n a hundred years – they thought I were crackers when I told 'em that.' He paused, shifting his throbbing legs, then added: 'There ain't no problem with being black, mate. It's all in *your* head, and in the heads of all the other white people ... that's where the trouble is. Then you makes trouble for us.'

There was a long blank silence which was broken by a paroxysm of coughing which left Cyril doubled up where he lay on the hard floor. It didn't diminish, but went on and on, driving the attention away from Lucas.

'I don't like the sound of that.' Stan uncoiled from his blanket, going to him. 'Here, mate ... you all right?'

Cyril was awake, but the only answer was a fresh bout of harsh coughing.

'He's spitting blood,' Stan said.

Norman was on his feet. 'D'you think I should give the guard a shout? He sounds as if he's going to choke and we've got no water.'

'It's worth a try. Chalky might be on duty,' Lucas said, watching Stan help Cyril into a sitting position.

The coughs were subsiding as Norman went to the door and rattled it, calling out. Two bright spots of red lay on the green sea of Cyril's face as he gasped against Stan's shoulder.

'He oughter be in hospital,' Lucas said.

'Never should've called him up y'mean,' Stan growled.

Norman shouted again, banging on the door with his fist.

From outside came a muffled shouted warning to 'Stop yer sniffin' racket!'

Cyril wheezed out: 'I'll ... be all ... right. Just give us ... a sec ...'

It was a brave self-deception and they all knew it. The effort of speaking had clearly exhausted him and he closed his eyes, all his remaining energy going into his strenuous breathing.

'We'd better take turns sitting with him,' Lucas said urgently. 'That lot out there ain't going to help.' He caught Stan's eye and knew what was in his mind. 'Stick together. Is that right, Stan – stick together?'

'On the nail!' Stan laughed softly. 'I'll make a socialist of you in spite of yerself, lad.'

'I wouldn't bet on it,' Lucas replied equally softly. 'I'm a solitary sod.'

Steady monotonous drizzle had turned the world into a grey soggy mist-ridden blurr. Standing in front of the officer's desk, Lucas watched the ever-changing pattern of water channelling down the uncurtained window. It helped to keep his mind off what might happen next. Ever since the sergeant had bawled:

'Sir, the prisoner, SIR!'

as he was marched into the room between an unknown corporal and Chalky White, he had stood in lengthening silence. He knew it was a calculated method to make him nervous. But knowing didn't make it any easier. He wondered again how Cyril was since they had taken him to hospital, and what had happened to Stan who was the first to be interviewed. Norman was waiting in the passage with only rumours for company.

And rumours were rife.

'Dartmoor and the treadmill party, mate. That's yer ticket ... Shoved down a mineshaft, *I* heard! They've taken over some disused ones Derby way ... Classed as loonies, that's what happens to conchies; straightjackets a regular thing ... Here, I heard about a feller as had to stand all day in a pit he'd dug hisself...'

Endless stories and whispers day after day. They were almost harder to bear than being knocked about.

'Knight, eh?'

Instinctively Lucas felt his muscles tighten and back go rigid at the bland ring of authority. His second reaction was to slouch in defiance. He looked across the desk at the young cherubic face that suggested a choirboy rather than a lieutenant. Only the eyes, a hard light blue, were disconcerting. They made him feel as exposed and helpless as a herring on a fishmonger's slab.

'Well, Knight, I hear you have not seen fit to mend your ways.' The voice continued deceptively mild.

Lucas said nothing; suspicion and uncertainty mingling.

The lieutenant rose up, a smooth cat-like movement, and went to look out of the window. Lucas stared at the small head, long neck, narrow back – a cut-out shape in charcoal against the grey rain-spattered oblong.

'Take off your clothes!' The order came crisply enough, but with an edge of jollity, as if they were sharing in some strange game.

Lucas was startled, but had the presence of mind not to move.

'Of course, if you refuse,' there was a hint of glee now, 'then these obliging chaps will give you a helping hand. What d'you say?'

Lucas did not budge.

'You 'eard the orficer. Strip!' The sergeant's voice lashed out.

Lucas continued to ignore the command and saw the officer pivot round then back again, as if the game was a curious version of Grandmother's Steps. Well, he could amuse himself all he wanted, stare and joke, strip him to the skin and force on that uniform lying in wait on the table, but it wouldn't make a bit of difference. No fighting. No violence. Just take it off again nice and quiet – that's what he'd do.

'Still refusing? Can't say I have an inkling how you chaps' minds work. You simply haven't a hope of winning. Besides, do you want to see your home and country overrun by the Bosche? Think what would happen to your mother and sisters; to your girl . . . have you a girl?'

For the first time Lucas spoke. 'No, nor a mother.'

'SIR!' barked the sergeant.

'And I ain't set on winning nothink, just doing what I sees as right.'

'SIR! Say Sir and no insolence!' The sergeant bristled indignation and threats.

'All right, Sergeant, he's making his own bed of nails.' The blue eyes examined Lucas, working from head to the flapping toes of his old worn-out boots. The smile that stretched his mouth failed to reach those eyes and the contrast left Lucas uneasy.

'You refuse?'

'Yes.'

'Very well. Sergeant!'

'Corporal Jarvis, Private White ... attenSHUN ... two steps forward and to the right ... Prisoner's clothes ORF!'

He didn't resist, but they took a delight in rending his shirt, shoving him so that he almost fell over as they jerked down his trousers and broke the knotted laces of his boots. He was left barefoot and shivering in nothing more than his vest and underpants.

'Uniform ON!' bawled the sergeant.

They tried very hard, but he was equally determined, and as fast as they buttoned the khaki shirt, he unbuttoned it. They tried one man holding his arms as the other lifted a foot and pushed on one trouser leg, but he managed to stand on the seat of the trousers so it was impossible to get his second foot started on its journey through the khaki tunnel. After five minutes of hot perspiring effort the sergeant joined in. An agonizing pressure was applied to his shoulder-blades as his arms were forced unnaturally back. Somebody kneed him in the base of the spine and then kicked his bare heel forward.

He was covered and buttoned inside two minutes.

'Sir ... the prisoner, sir!'

But Lucas had started on his shirt buttons again. He'd just reached the third from the bottom when the lieutenant said with mild astonishment:

'You Absolutists take the biscuit. Last chap was just the same. Masochists the lot of you.'

'I ain't an Absolutist. I wanted to join the Non-Combatant

Corps, but nobody would listen.' The words fell from him before he could check them, but he didn't care. He'd speak his mind once and for all.

'Silence!' roared the sergeant.

'No . . . wait a minute, Sergeant. Let me get this straight. You want to join the Non-Combatants, do you?'

'Yes . . . sir.' Lucas stared at the floor.

'Don't you understand that they wear uniforms like all army corps? Refusing to do so blocks any chance you have of joining them.' The lieutenant had seated himself at the desk again and began to play with a pencil, doodling on the back of a piece of paper. He took time drawing a circle which spiralled inwards. He didn't look up or speak. When he did, Lucas had finished unbuttoning his shirt but had got no further. They eyed one another.

'I'll make you an offer,' said the lieutenant. 'Accept the uniform and I will see that you are sent to the Non-Combatant Corps in France.'

Behind him the sergeant made a curious noise which he altered into a cough. Which to choose . . . yes or no . . . should he . . . shouldn't he? There was no way of knowing. All he could recognize was a small hole that promised escape. But escape to France. Hurry hurry or the chance would vanish . . . Which . . . which . . .

'Well?' There was an edge of impatience. A loss of geniality.

There was no choice after all. With a flash of insight Lucas recognized it had been like that all along. Keeping the truth at arm's length. Hiding – that's what he had been doing. Being a coward. With a climax of self-disgust, he tore off the shirt and threw it on the ground.

15

THE knock on the front door was not one Bella recognized. The very fact that it was the front door was a little unnerving. Neighbours, if they came at all, used the area steps. The usual postwoman had a very personal knock – two long, two short. This could be a different post. It had a certain tentative authority.

'Ain't you going to see who it is?' Lily asked, sprinkling a quantity of salt on her porridge. 'I'd go meself only them stairs and me legs don't go together.'

Bella got up feeling her stomach constrict. Suppose it was one of those telegrams? They hadn't heard from Jack in ages. She took a deep breath. 'Give me a cupper tea to take and I'll go up to the Admiral after.'

Lily poured the tea without comment. Both knew they were holding the same thought in their minds. It was a commonplace fear but none the less acute and worrying for that. Taking the mug, Bella opened the door to the stairs, hesitating as if she was about to speak. Lily smiled. There was nothing to say after all, Bella decided. The security of Lily's presence was heart-warming. Turning, she went up to the ground-floor room which opened directly on to the street and put the mug down on the bottom step of the second staircase before unlatching the door.

'Hello Bella,' Catherine Ashe said. 'I'm so glad to catch you. I was afraid you would be at work.'

The initial surprise at seeing such an unexpected visitor changed to faint embarrassment as she saw Catherine looking at the smudge on the door where the red paint had been. The task of removing every trace of the damning letters had been impossible. Bella stood back and said hurriedly: 'Won't you come in?' As Catherine passed her she caught a lingering spicy scent, like the smell of cedarwood pencils, and saw with a small shock how Catherine had aged. Bella remembered her as thin, but now her Barathea coat hung loose and her deepset eyes seemed to have sunk further into her skull, but her walk and speech were as brisk as ever. When Bella had shut the door she said:

'It's a long time since we saw each other. How are you?'

'Mustn't grumble,' Bella said. 'How's yerself?'

'Well enough.' Catherine shrugged off the inquiry. 'I know you must be wondering why I am here and I won't beat about the bush. I've had news of Lucas ... and Norman.'

'Where is he? What's happened? Is he all right?' Bella couldn't cage the questions and felt her heart pumping sickly in her throat.

'He's alive I can tell you that much, but I haven't further details of his health. All I can tell you is that they've been sent to France.'

'*France!*' Bella stood very still trying to suppress all the rumours and gossip she had gleaned about conchies in the past weeks. The amount was formidable. The stories alarming. The worst of all was the death trap of France.

'That's it then,' she said bleakly.

'What are you thinking?' Catherine was puzzled.

Ice seemed to have entered her veins making her cold through and through. It was probably as well – freezing her emotions.

'Bella?' Catherine caught her hand.

The touch was surprisingly warm. Like a reminder of spring-time, so close now. Easter very soon and in the country primroses would be out. Luke would never see primroses again.

'Bella!' Catherine was shaking her hand. 'You'd better sit down. What *is* it?'

'They don't return do they? Shot in the back I heard. Never given a chance.'

Catherine pushed her into one of the horsehair chairs. 'Now then, I don't know what tall stories you've been told. Whatever they are I suggest you throw them out of the window and listen to a few facts. Last lot of COs who were sent to France caused such a rumpus in Parliament that they were brought back double-quick. I grant you that a death sentence hung over them for a while, but it won't ever happen again. Of course no more batches of COs were supposed to be sent abroad, but it isn't always easy to stop some of these high-up officers who fancy themselves as God making decisions contrary to official orders. But the important thing to remember is that the N–CF know what's happened and we aren't without influence. There's no chance that they will be quietly shot. I don't say they won't have a bad time and I can't predict when they'll arrive back in England, but you and I haven't the right to sit down meekly and give up hope ... stop fighting.'

People were always telling her she should fight ... *she* kept telling herself. But really what good did it do? What would be, would be. Luke was no longer on English soil. Catherine could talk till Christmas and it wouldn't make the slightest difference.

'You ... you said Norman as well.' Bella pulled herself together with an effort. 'That's yer nephew ain't it?'

'Yes, but he's more like a brother. We're in the same boat you and I.'

'Like them.' It was poor comfort, but better than nothing. Did this woman with her hollowed-out face and blown white hair feel that too? Bella scrutinized her, trying to decide, and their eyes met. Catherine barely smiled, but there was a lift at the corners of her rather precise mouth and the effect was a gear shift in Bella's thinking. Her mind cleared and she felt a touch of shame at being so wrapped in her own desperation. After all she wasn't the only one. Catherine must be suffering too – was suffering. Her face said that.

'However did you find out?' Bella asked.

'You aren't going to believe this.'

'Well what?'

Catherine continued: 'One of the prisoners managed to drop a note out of the train on the way to the boat. Written on the back of a cigarette packet. Chance in a million that it would ever be picked up, but it was. Luckily he managed to chuck it out of the window when they were moving slowly through a station.'

Chance in a million was right. Bella felt a small rising of hope. If that could come off, then maybe there was a chance in a million for Luke? She tried not to let the hope swell too much. The let-down was always worse.

'Is there anythink I can do?' she asked.

'Not much for your brother directly at present, but a great deal for the N–CF if you've the time and inclination. But I thought you were working in munitions with your friend?'

'Was.' Bella didn't want the bother of explaining the factory ructions. 'Emmie's nursing now. She's a VAD and I've got a job in a Music Hall the Elephant way, as dogsbody. At the cash desk, bit of sewing, dresser, bit of cleaning, things like that. But I don't have to start till eleven and there ain't no clocking in. The hours are long because of the evening performances. Mr Nash ain't a slave driver though he does like you to put in yer hours, but he won't blow up if yer late for any reason.' She could see that Catherine was surprised but too polite to comment. She was still surprised at herself for taking the job, though she told herself it was a temporary measure while the Admiral was ill. When he was fit enough for Lily to cope, she'd be off. She asked: 'What sort of thing?' tentative because guilt was still strong and held her back.

'Messenger work mostly. Of course there are people who take on more.' Catherine paused and Bella felt obliged to prompt:

'Like what?'

'Helping people who are resisting conscription. Giving them house room – the sort of help your brother received.'

Well she'd asked for it! But surely Catherine wasn't suggesting she should have conchies *here*? The Admiral would have a fit and even Lily might dig in her heels. Bella realized with astonishment that she was arguing with herself as if she was seriously considering the prospect. She also realized that Catherine was expecting some sort of comment, and said hastily:

‘I dunno as I could do anythink like that, but I’ll think it over and let you know,’ feeling a chill of apprehension in case she had committed herself too far. At the same moment Lily called from the foot of the stairs:

‘Are you there, our Bel? Who was it?’

‘Oh Lord, the tea! It’ll be stone cold.’ Bella jumped up and collected the mug. ‘I’m supposed to be taking it up. Me Grandad’s in bed poorly.’

‘Nothing serious I hope?’ Catherine said.

‘Old age mostly, but nothink else that ain’t curable.’

Catherine straightened her coat. ‘I’d better go. It’s been good meeting you again.’ She held out her hand.

Bella swapped the mug from one hand to the other, awkwardly accepting. ‘Ever so kind of you to take the trouble to come all this way.’

‘It was the least I could do. Like we said before – we’re in the same boat. There’s an easing when trouble is shared.’ Catherine tightened her grip as if to add weight to her words, then let go and went to the door. ‘We’ll be meeting again I know, so it’s *au revoir*.’

‘Tata … and thanks.’ Bella watched as she went down the steps, and saw her turn briefly to wave before walking purposefully along the street. The door shut again, Bella called: ‘Just someone with a message, Lil. I’ll be down directly,’ going on up the second flight to the Admiral’s room where she paused for a moment before entering and taking a full breath to make sure she would act unruffled. She didn’t want him asking questions; stumbling on to the facts about Luke which were hovering in the forefront of her mind and liable to slip out if she didn’t watch herself. Talk of Luke always upset him.

The sun was seeping in through the brown threadbare curtains, filling the room with a dingy glow. Setting the mug on the washstand by the bed she went to draw them, saying cheerily:

‘Morning, Grandad. Did you sleep a bit better last night?’

Light spilled across the dusty floorboards, over the faded rag-rug and on to the rumpled quilt. No answer. He was certainly out for the count. Usually by now he was stirring. Bella went back to the bed. The silence was suddenly a forceful presence and she leaned over his bulk, twitching the bedclothes from his face.

She said: 'Grandad!' without any sound, seeing eyes and mouth open, tongue slightly protruding, a line of saliva like a silver slug-track drying on the muddy black skin of his cheek. She knew he was dead and wanted to touch him but couldn't because of what she might feel and because there was a change in his face. It was no longer the face she had known and loved all her life, but a stranger's. She continued to bend over him, the first smacking shock filling her with panic and a child-like resentment. He'd no right to go away and leave her. The panic faded and was replaced by the single chilling thought – I'm free. It ought to have brought shame, but there was no room for anything except an immense iron-cold aching sense of loss.

No more rumbustious laughter.

No more red cocked hat.

No more jellied eels and stout on a Saturday night.

No more stories of Midnight and Jess.

No more Admiral.

The past seemed finally closed.

Very carefully Bella picked up the mug of cold tea and left the bedside. She couldn't bring herself to straighten the quilt, neither did she want to redraw the curtains. The Admiral had always favoured daylight. At the door she paused and looked back at the still mound in the bed. She had never felt so alone or missed Luke so much. Every secure thing she had known seemed to be crumbling into dust, leaving her a solitary scare-crow figure, to be stared at by the world. It was unbearable. An agony. She jerked back from the terror of it and, forgetting to be quiet, rushed from the room calling for Lily.

16

WOULD the journey never end? Lucas stared across the twilight landscape from the back of the uncovered Ford van. There were five of them and a couple of guards. Three Objectors and two soldiers, who'd been loaded in at a brief stop somewhere between Boulogne and this nowhere nightmare place. He'd not yet discovered why the soldiers were there or what they'd done. Everyone was silent and glum. He did know they were prisoners – like himself, Stan and Norman Ashe. And that was the only bit of luck in the whole business – the three of them staying together after all. There was a moment on the embarkation train at Victoria Station when he'd thought he was on his tod. The relief when Stan and Norman with two other Objectors from up North were pushed in, almost as the train was on the move, had been colossal. The journey to France would have been a treat if the end of it hadn't been so much of a threat. They'd joked, swapped stories, shared some bread and bully beef. Even the guards had been decent – giving them fags and chatting.

The van jolted violently over a particularly large pothole in the scarred road. They slithered dangerously towards the deep mud which sucked at the edges either side. In the distance was the thunder of guns. Lucas saw Stan's head bounce against the canvas hood covering the driving seat. For the first time in over an hour he opened his eyes as one of the guards ripped out a string of ripe words.

'How d'you do it?' Lucas muttered.

'What?'

'Sleep.'

Stan yawned and eased his cramped legs, scratching under the muffler wound round his neck. 'I can sleep on a clothes line.

Always could. You'll come to it with practice.' He peered across the undulating mud stretching into the distance that was peppered with splintered tree stumps and an occasional ruined farm building. A dark line almost on the horizon marked a strip of railway and beyond that the charcoal sky was lit with a sudden glare of orange and purple flame. It hung for a minute and then drifted downwards, accompanied by a great thundering roar which didn't die but changed into louder gunfire.

'Kite balloon's copped it . . . poor buggers.' The guard shifted the rifle between his knees.

'Fools y'means don't yer?' The second guard wiped a hand across his lined face. 'Sitting ducks and they knows it.'

Lucas shivered, partly from the knife-edge wind that cut through the threadbare coat (thrust at him on leaving Henriville barracks) and partly from a too vivid picture of a furnace of flames round his shrinking body with nothing but empty space below. He felt horror and wondered at such misguided bravery. Sitting ducks all right! And for what? A possible view behind enemy lines. He'd learned their purpose soon after they'd landed at Boulogne. He'd also learned that where Kite balloons were tethered, the front line was not far away. He shivered again and simultaneously a whine followed by a deafening explosion plugged his ears and sent him slithering to the floor of the van on top of the others, trembling with fright.

The first guard yelled out to the driver who had increased speed: 'How much further, Charlie?'

If there was an answer, nobody heard. A second ear-shattering bang split the air, after it a shower of mud and thick rolling acrid smoke.

'We oughter stop, Charlie . . . stop can't yer?'

The first guard elbowed his mate. 'Whatcher got – a death wish?'

Next to Lucas as they crouched on the floor, one of the soldier-prisoners began snivelling and hiccupping snatches of prayer under cover of the guns. Lucas dared raise his head and met the eyes of the second soldier-prisoner.

'Those shells?'

'Yep ... whizz-bangs.' His face broke into a curious almost cruel smile. 'They weren't nothing. You'll find out.'

The van careered along the worsening surface which was turning from metalled road to rutted track. Breathless and with his stomach in knots, Lucas could only hunch as low as possible; unable to see where they were going; trying not to give way to mounting fear. It seemed an eternity before the van slowed and came to a stop.

'Let's be having yer. Out ... OUT!'

They scrambled awkwardly from the van, their limbs numb and unresponsive. The light had almost gone. Lucas's first reaction was that he'd stepped into another planet. Or a dream. Out of the mud rose a mound of rubble topped by two monstrous solitary shapes poking into the sky. There were no trees, no houses, no habitation of any kind that he could recognize. A few carts bunched near the rubble, but the only true human element was a small group of soldiers.

'Prisoners?' one was saying. 'What ludicrous nonsense is this? I've had no instructions ... no message of any kind.'

'Information dispatched at thirteen ought fifteen hours last Tuesday, sir.'

The guard was ramrod stiff, which meant that the tired grimy bloke in the balaclava, knitted at least one size too big for him, must be an officer. Lucas heard him make a sound of exasperation.

'What crass nincompoop thought that one up? Five did you say, Sergeant? *Five?*'

'Yessir.'

'My God what the hell did they think I was going to do with them even if I had received the message? We're only a mile or so from the front, man. I haven't got time to wet-nurse a bunch of cowards that shot themselves in the feet or whatever it was. What do they think goes on at the front?'

The guard didn't attempt to answer. Lucas saw Norman and Stan look at one another and then at him. The soldier-prisoners stared fixedly at the ground. The bloke was right – Lucas thought – it was a case of passing the buck. They were nothing more than useless lumber. They wants you dead, son, he told himself. All on us. That way we'll be out of their hair.

'Get 'em in the trench, Sergeant, and put a man to guard them.' The officer's voice was tight with fatigue and barely suppressed anger. 'I'll deal with them when I can.'

The rain had begun again. A fine drenching drizzle, and as Lucas clambered down the ladder and arrived on the slimy duckboards his feet went from under him, landing him on his knees. He got up, seeing planks lining the trench; supporting sandbags; vague tented shapes of soldiers draped in groundsheets.

The officer had disappeared through a doorway curtained with sacking into the dugout behind and the sergeant followed after selecting a guard. Norman was last but one in the line of damp prisoners. He had his shoulders hunched against the rain.

'What d'you think they'll do with us?' Lucas asked him.

'When they've sorted out our crimes, give us appropriate punishment jobs.' Norman sounded surprisingly lighthearted.

'Like what?'

'Errands of one kind or another. Where the most danger is.'

The guard overheard. 'Y'can be sniffin' certain of that!' He propped himself against the side of the trench. 'Sniffin' shirkers! Making me stand out here with a bunch like you when I could be snug in me billet. Can't even light a fag!'

'They'll separate us, y'know that,' Stan warned quietly. 'They'll not want us to support each other. But whatever happens, don't forget there's plenty back in Blighty working on our behalf.'

'They don't know we're in France.' Cold conviction thinned Lucas's determination, leaving him in a fresh pit of depression. This switchback process was becoming more frequent; more difficult to control.

Norman pulled his coat collar higher, shielding his mouth

with his hand. 'I wouldn't say that. Remember when we slowed down going through the tail end of London? Couldn't make out the station name, but I managed to scribble a note and chuck it on to the platform.'

Lucas couldn't really believe that a scrap of paper littering a platform would be picked up and delivered – Norman must be crackers! But you had to hang on to something. Perhaps that's all it was – hope. A flimsy priceless thread of hope. His own hope was in his boots. All he could do was wait and see how right Norman's guess was.

He found out next morning.

They had spent the night on the hard cold floor of one of a number of tunnels honeycombing a bank some little distance from the first trench. With no blankets and no food in him, Lucas had slept fitfully. Each time he woke there had been a sound of thunder. But whether it was thunder or guns, he couldn't be sure. The echo merged with his dreams and he was still trying to sort it out when a voice shouted:

'Move yerselves y'lazy sods.'

The boot in Lucas's ribs brought him to his feet, his head still muzzy with sleep. He looked at the corporal, a wiry sharp-featured man with scrubbing-brush ginger hair.

'You two!' The corporal picked out the soldier-prisoners. 'Smarten up. Captain Hastings wants to see you. The rest stay here.'

Lucas tried out the tender spot on his ribs as the soldiers were led away. He avoided looking at anyone while he tried to gather and bring order to his inner self. It wasn't easy and the hard-won control almost slipped away when the ginger corporal re-appeared and focused on him.

'Sod me! Here, Ticker ... come over a minute. We've got a bleedin' nigger. I've only just realized. Now ain't that a turn up?'

Ticker, a bundle of ill-fitting khaki surmounted by a perfectly round bald head, emerged from a cranny in the wall-planks like a woodlouse. He was blinking and staring through red-rimmed eyes. 'Blimey, yer right! Hang on a minute, George. I'll get Boxer. He'll want to see.'

'All right, but get a move on or I'll be on fatigues for keeping his Nibs waiting.'

Lucas busied himself tucking his shirt back in his trousers and rubbing his hands over his face – trying to rid himself of nervous apprehension and the last clinging traces of sleep. Norman and Stan were doing much the same. He wished fervently the day would get properly started, instead of drifting into another of these endless delays. His resolution to take each moment as it came – savouring the quiet times and enduring the injustice and danger – stirred and sank as he heard Ticker's voice, squeaky and insistent, coming round the corner of the tunnel:

'Here he is, Boxer. See I weren't having yer on.'

Lucas saw Ticker first, but he wasn't of any importance because the man he had gone to fetch was Jack. Thinner than before, but still like a barn door. The shock cancelled Lucas's power to think rationally. His head felt bursting with fragments from a lifetime, and he looked to Jack as he had always looked to him in order to find out what he was supposed to do. The old pull and resistance exerted their familiar strengths, pushing him even further back into the long ago yesterdays. For the first time Jack returned his gaze, and with a concentration of emotions that Lucas recognized from years of living together. Disgust, love, anger, pity, scorn, embarrassment were all present, but there was something else as well. Something new. The tough confident expression had been replaced by a restless haunted look – as if he were pursued by ghosts. It had the resignation of a bitter old man which wrung Lucas because it was the opposite of all he knew to be Jack. He waited to be acknowledged, but all that Jack said was:

'All right, so I've seen him. You weren't lying so I shan't have to punch yer head, Ticker. Now can I go and have me nosh in peace?'

Ticker looked crestfallen. 'Thought you might've known him,

Boxer. Yer the only two darkies we've seen, ain't they, George?'

'That's right,' George confirmed.

They both looked at Jack hopefully, but he only shrugged and turned away, walking back along the tunnel with a positive wooden stride. Lucas recognized that as well. Another sure sign of embarrassment. He watched him go with a sense of desolation so absolute that he could neither move, nor speak.

'Come on then, y'sniffin' rosebuds. There's a treat in store. Yer going to be given the once over by real big brass. Colonel Briggs-Heston! He don't like conchies. He hates conchies. Has 'em for breakfast, and then served up on toast with his good-night rum.' Corporal George was enjoying himself. 'In line then ... get moving,' helping Lucas – still slow with shock – with a painful kick on the leg.

'Were these all the prisoners, Corporal?'

'No, sir. Two more, sir. Privates Wisley and Cashmore were here last night, sir.'

'Well, where are they now?'

'Sent to the front line with the relief company early this morning, sir.'

'Hmm!'

So this skeleton with rat-trap mouth and glossy Sam Browne, sitting at the trestle-table with that crazy potted geranium in front of him; claw fingers picking and shredding strips of paper – this was big brass! Lucas's anger, roused by being kicked, had cooled and hardened into iron determination. He'd take rations up the line, help with wounded, but he would not wear uniform nor touch a gun nor even carry messages of war.

Colonel Briggs-Heston looked through and beyond the three prisoners.

'Conscientious Objection may be accepted across the channel in England. It is not so in France. You are now in the war zone. The enemy line is close at hand. Our own front closer still. You will do whatever you are told, or be shot. Is that clear?'

Silence was his answer.

He turned on the corporal, nailing him with an unblinking stare. 'Why are these men still without uniform and arms?'

The corporal was rigid, eyes fixed on the end of the dugout. 'Sir, they refuses to put on uniform, sir. And Captain Hastings ordered them not to be given arms, sir.'

'In God's name why not?'

'Sir – in case they shot theirselves, sir.'

'And where are the nearest stores?'

'Dominion Camp, sir.'

The parchment skin did not change colour, but Lucas detected a slight tightening of the already grim jaw muscles. He felt his guts weaken as his own determination became more rock-like.

'Then they have made their final choice.' The voice was cold and dismissive. He scrutinized them again in a detached way and Lucas thought – we might just as well be cattle for the slaughter house. He slid a glance at Stan and Norman who stood shoulder to shoulder beside him, his eyes irresistibly drawn on to the pointing claw which flicked down with each pronouncement.

'Field punishment number one ...' Stan.

'Front line ...' Oh Gawd – himself!

'Death by firing squad ...'

'No,' Lucas said loudly and without thought for himself. 'What's he done more'n us? That ain't right. That's *injustice*!'

'And if that man is unfortunate enough to return,' the voice was clipped now; honed sharp with freezing anger, 'let him suffer the same end. Shoot him!'

Twelve muddled fragmented hours after the colonel had pronounced sentence, they were dispatched to the front. Lucas had lost count of time. They seemed to have been marching for days. Already the noise was menacing. It came in bursts – the boom and crunch of heavy artillery, rapid machine-gun chatter, interspersed with the screams of high explosive shells. Afterwards, a listening silence broken only by sounds of men squelching breathily across the muddy field. In the first light they could see the remains of a village scattering its ruined walls across the street.

'Where's this place?' Lucas asked.

'This?' Ticker pulled at his pack, moving the gasmask in order to scratch underneath. ''Alf a mile from 'ell I shouldn't wonder.'

'It'll be Voormezeele south of Wipers if we ain't lost,' Corporal George said, lowering his rifle. 'Which is 'ell, or will be when we gets to the front.'

'Ypres,' Norman corrected in an undertone.

Corporal George heard. 'Wipers I said and Wipers I meant, Mr Bloody Knowall Conchie.'

'Go it Corp ... you tell the bleeders ... what d'they want to bring trash like that along for ... can't you fire accidental like, Corp? Save us all trouble ...' Spurts of laughter mingled with acid remarks as the restless waiting soldiers bunched round them.

The Battalion had paused for the officers – Captain Hastings among them – to take bearings. Lucas was faintly glad that this particular captain was there. Because of him Stan had *not* been condemned to lie spreadeagled on a gun carriage, and Norman had escaped the firing squad. Big Brass, it seemed, did not always have the last say. Not that being sent to the front line was in any way a better experience, but at least it would be shared.

A buzz of communication travelled through the waiting men.

'Get moving,' said Corporal George, raising his rifle again, 'and no daft ideas, or you won't have a gnat's chance of keepin' on breathin'.'

The lines of men moved left, descending into a long communication trench signposted 'Estaminet Lane' which wound muddy and endless, bringing them to another sign 'Old French Trench', where a good portion of the men remained as reserve support. Captain Hastings's company was not among them. It marched on through other trenches with crazier names – 'Old Kent Road' ... 'Long Chicken' ... 'Sniper's Cop'. The noise of war was constant. The smell inescapable. Lucas wondered how long it would be before he stopped a bullet, and felt sick with fear.

'Captain Hastings is hit. And the Sarge. The whole bloody bunch has gone.'

'Put a sock in it, Ticker!'

The eyes, red holes in a black face, stared. Ticker gulped. 'The blokes down the other end dunno what to do. The parapet's gone and the machine gun. Half the trench has caved in. Sparker and Brown are wounded. You'll have to come, George. There ain't nobody else.'

Lucas pressed against the bottom of the trench with the mud and rotting stench, head pounding with noise ... bursting with noise. Gun noise; shouting; shrieks ...

'Bloody 'ell, George, what's stopping yer?'

'This lot.'

'Stuff 'em!'

'Captain said ...'

'Captain's dead.'

Another deafening salvo and an enfilade of bullets ricocheted from the tilted corrugated-iron roof of a mangled dugout where part of a corpse protruded.

'George!' Ticker yelled.

'All *right*!' The corporal opened his gullet and poured the last dregs of a bottle of rum down it, getting to unsteady feet. Beneath him the broken duckboard jack-knifed. He stumbled forward, desperately trying to save his rifle from the mud, grabbing at it and tightening his hands.

There was an ear-cracking sound as the rifle went off.

On his knees in the mud Lucas looked up and saw everything in precise detail. Disbelief in Ticker's burned-out eyeholes as his body was punched backwards; Ticker's mouth an O of gurgling blood, the gaping wound at the base of his throat a scarlet fountain; Stan and Norman flattening themselves against the sandbags; George outlined against a pearly sky brightened even more by Very flares, the barbed wire behind framing his head like a halo. All imprinted forever. Nothing could erase it. Only death.

The explosion that followed came with a sheet of light, vibrating the ground and throwing up monstrous clods of earth and rubble. Lucas felt a stunning blow at the back of his skull which made another instantaneous explosion inside his head. A kaleidoscope of coloured lights flashed in front of his eyes just before he catapulted into darkness.

When he drifted back to consciousness the sky was black not pearl. Stars like so many brand new tanners. He seemed to be floating towards them. Perhaps he could pick a handful, fill his pockets, be a rich man. He'd buy Bella that blue dress with the neck frill she'd fancied so much. The stars were turning, turning ... or was it his head? Stone. Sandstone. Granite. Purbeck Marble. All the names Stan had learned him.

Stan!

He was suddenly clearheaded. That was Froggy sky up there. Froggy ground under him. He became acutely aware of three things simultaneously. A great weight lying across his stomach. Hammering pain in his head. The moment of Ticker's death. He drew in a sharp breath and tried to move the weight, his hands coming in contact with wet stickiness which became harder, then pulpy, then sharp. With a jerk of horror he pulled back, realizing he had touched flesh and naked bone. The air was putrid.

A choking groan and a harsh whispered: 'Mother!'

He called sharply: 'Stan? Where are you?' But the only answer was another groan which hissed and bubbled and which he tried to locate by calling out again. No answer. Christ, if there was only some light! He didn't even know what night this was or how long they had been here. His head was heavy with pain, tempting him to lie still. Not bother. But there was Stan to find. And Norman. He began picking away at slimy earth and stones, lacerating his hands on invisible barbed wire. But keeping on and on, desperate to be free. The utter darkness almost defeated him. He felt as if he was the only person left alive in the whole world. Even the sound of gunfire would have been welcome instead of this deafening silence. Terror rose up and he called out:

'Stan ... Stan!'

The awful groaning began once more, dissolving into a low mutter. It seemed to be coming from somewhere over to the left. With a tremendous effort Lucas wriggled from beneath the weight of dead man and rubble.

'Mother – mother – mother ...' on and on.

Lucas said sharply: 'Stan are you hit?'

'Mother ... mother ...'

'Stan, tell me ... where did they get you? Can you move?'

There was no reply except a gurgling cough which ended abruptly in silence, leaving him paralysed until the groaning began again. He called out:

'For Gawd's sake I'm coming, don't move,' making for the direction of the sound. His head was being pumped up like a colossal football bladder. He felt horribly sick and dizzy, but he kept going, inching along. Groping through slime. Finding a hand. In his disturbed state he wanted to hold it because he thought it was Stan's, but it was stiff and cold, and not attached to any arm. The shock raised skeletons of terror and he shouted Stan's name over and over. As the panic subsided to a level where he could think he found he was sweating and trembling, and to defeat the ghoul began to talk as if Stan was listening.

'We ain't gonners yet. I'll get us out. Hang on ... just hang on. All we've got to do is hang on.' He could crawl again now and dragged over the wreckage of bodies until he touched live flesh, feeling across shoulders, neck, face – all of which seemed undamaged. Stan was lying on his back, that much Lucas discovered. He wanted to find out where the wound was, but it was impossible in the darkness and he was afraid of hurting him. All he could recognize was quantities of congealing blood gouting from Stan's left side. He felt the bile rise in his throat and for some time could do nothing. The dreadful muttering began again.

'Field dressings,' Lucas said. 'There must be some amongst this lot. The dead don't need them.' His head was swimming and it seemed immensely important to make a practical effort. He explored with his hands, hoping to contact a small oiled package, but it was hopeless. Stan's breathing had become a dry rattle.

'I won't leave you. I'll stay with you. It'll be all right.' Lucas slid his hand down Stan's arm until he found the chilled hand which he grasped and held, trying to warm it back into life. The pounding in his head swelled and his ears roared. A sudden sharp scent of oranges was there and then he slid back into unconsciousness.

The sun came up and went down. Guns boomed. The chatter of machine guns flew alongside a flock of small birds, black against a quilted springtime sky. There were other live things. Bronzed flies. And a rat cleaning its whiskers. Lucas saw him briefly in a moment of consciousness, as he saw the sky, blue, and another time, smoky grey. He was clotted with thirst and thought he ought to do something about finding water, but then the blackness came again. It was parted next by a small dancing luminous moth, which wasn't a moth but the cupped light of a torch. Voices swam into his ears and a sharp pain stabbed him in the small of the back. He shifted and groaned.

'Christ! Over here, Pozzo. Under this lot.'

'Nobody could live under there, mate.'

'They are. I ain't deaf.'

The small light made moons through Lucas's closed eyelids. With a great effort he opened them.

The same voice said: 'Christ!' again.

Lucas tried to smile, but it never got going. He whispered: 'Jack! You always missed ... the tram ... lazy ... bastard ...' He saw his brother's face come close, the shape of it cut into strong pits and hollows by torchlight, and felt himself being lifted. The pain had gone from his head, but he couldn't hang on to his thoughts. They slithered from him downhill into grasping darkness.

17

BACKSTAGE the theatre was in a ferment. Nothing unusual in that, Bella thought, pushing the dressing-room door shut with her foot. There was always some panic. From the stage drifted the sound of a strong nasal voice:

'KKKKatie ... KKKKatie ...
You're the one and only girl that I adore ...'

Bella knew the pattern and sighed with relief. At least three more songs – time to take the weight off her trotters. The job was never dull but it wasn't a rest cure neither!

She sat down in the chair before the dressing table and reached for the paper. By a trick of gaslight the ghost of Lucas stared back at her from the darkened mirror. Face thinned and sculptured, the flesh pared down so that the ears stood out with more emphasis. She let out a small gasp, then told herself not to be an idiot. If Luke was a ghost as Lily believed, he wouldn't be one for haunting anybody. The apparition was her own reflection, hair scraped back so her ears showed. Didn't suit. She'd have to rearrange it. The firm common-sense thought didn't stop the trembling which came so often these days. She shook the paper open angry with herself, and read 'VOTES FOR WOMEN' but didn't take it in, her mind possessed by the march of memory. Eight months since the telegram and the formal letter announcing Jack's death. Ten since Luke had gone to France and vanished as completely as if he had never existed. All her persistence had been in vain. Not a word, not a whisper could she unearth about Luke. But even now she refused to believe, as Lily did, that he was dead.

She forced herself to reread the headline 'VOTES FOR

WOMEN' but was again interrupted, this time by a tap on the door, which opened and Lily came in breathing heavily.

'Blimey ... them stairs! Here, I've brought you a visitor, darlin'.'

'Emmie!' Bella dropped the paper and got up. 'Oh it's good to see you!'

'And yo, Bel.' Emily came close and hugged her. 'It seems an age since last time.'

'It is an age. Months.' Bella hugged her in return.

'We met at the stage door,' Lily said, sitting down and easing her feet out of her shoes.

'Didn't know you were coming tonight.'

Lily picked up the paper, shaking out the creases. 'Neither did I, darlin'. It just come over me sitting on me tod in front of the fire. The Admiral's chair looked so empty. Lily gal – I says – time you was up and doing or you'll be a bath of tears. So I ups, and jolly glad I am or I'd've never got to meet yer friend. She's off to France she says.'

'Is that true?' Bella held Emily away.

'Yes ... it's one of the reasons I've come. To say good-bye.'

'When d'you go?'

'Monday.' Emily laughed, and in the gaslight Bella saw her eyes shining. In spite of herself she felt a touch of jealousy. Emmie's obvious excitement pointed up her own restless frame of mind and brought out the evergreen question that had been pursuing her since the Admiral died – Why don't I do something brave and worthwhile ... something needed? There's nothing to stop me now. It was ironic that Emily after all was the one to be going to France.

'You are lucky!' The words were out before she could stop them, and she saw both Emily and Lily staring at her in amazement.

'Dunno about lucky,' Emily said. 'I knows I feels much more settled and content since I've been nursing. Queer when yo thinks about it. I've seen some terrible sights ... wounded men ...' She left off speaking as if the horrors were too dreadful to describe. After a second, she continued: 'That's my other reason for coming. Vic.'

Bella reacted with spontaneous alarm. It showed in her face and her quick intake of breath.

'No . . . *no*! Wounded. Bad enough, but he's making progress. They've sent him home. He's in hospital in a place called Wedstock.'

'I knows Wedstock,' interrupted Lily. 'Used to visit me old Gran when she lived there. Nice little village in Kent with a real old-time pub called The Dun Cow.'

Emily nodded. 'That's it.'

'Won't take you long to get there on the bus, Bel. You'll be able to visit him easy.'

'Would yo?' Emily asked. 'He'd be that pleased.'

'Of course.' Bella felt heavy with relief and startled by the depth of her concern. It was more than she'd bargained for, and she didn't dare examine the feeling too closely.

Emily said diffidently: 'There's another thing. He said to say he's got something to tell yo about Luke.'

They gazed at each other, and Lily said:

'It ain't no good thinking like that, Bella. Yer a fool if you does.'

Bella pressed both fists against her rib-cage. 'I can't help what I feels here. I've never been able to believe he's dead. *Never!*'

'Just because you ain't seen the corpse with yer own eyes, you let yer fancy get the upper hand. You always was a dreamer,' Lily said harshly. She had let the paper slither to the floor and Emily picked it up.

'Vic's a crafty old devil. He shouldn't have . . .' Emily stopped, holding up the paper so that the light fell on it. 'Votes for women,' she read slowly – then breathy and excited: 'D'yo see? It's happened at last . . . after all that trying . . . all that struggle. We've got the vote, Bel. Think of it!' And shoving the paper at Lily, she caught hold of Bella's arms, whirling her round. 'The vote . . . we've got the vote!'

For the first time Bella realized what it was her eyes

had been reading without her mind understanding. Emily's boisterous joy was infectious, but she felt more in tune with Lily when she said:

'Took a war to do it. Not that I could ever see what all the fuss was about. Much good it'll do you and me. We ain't never going to end up in Parliament putting the world to rights – more's the pity. Wouldn't be no ruddy wars if we did.'

'Oh but we will.' There were tears swimming in Emily's eyes, and she gave Bella a small shake as if to push in her own ardent conviction. 'We ain't finished yet. Yo see!'

Bella smiled, not wanting to crush her enthusiasm, but unable to think of anything except the glorious chance that Luke was still alive. She was burning with renewed hope which was almost too precious, too fragile to grasp. The intensity of feeling reached out to the dressing room where she stood; every detail engraving itself on her mind. Peeling whitewash on the ceiling. The handmark where someone had leaned against the wall. A tawdry spangled costume hanging on a nail. Powder dust, sticks of make-up, a smeared rag, on the dressing table. Lily's fat wrinkled face and elaborate hennaed hair. Emily smiling . . . smiling. The audience was singing now. Every word coming to her water-clear:

'It's a long way to Tipperary,
It's a long way to go . . .'

and winding round the song, a warning hooter.

'My Gawd, Fritz is at it again,' Lily said. 'Well he can do as he pleases. If I've gotter go, I'd as soon cop it in here as anywhere. I'd feel more at home.'

The passion of feeling in Bella concentrated and changed to a burst of affection for this tough old trouper. She leaned over and kissed her. 'Me too!' Astonishingly it was true. It didn't matter that the place was grubby and smelled of stale grease-paint and the lingering odours of booze. She loved it all, she really did. Being different was normal here. The odd ones were outside.

'I ain't bothered neither,' Emily said. 'If your name's on the bomb it'll get yo. If not . . .' she shrugged.

Bella could hear the distant boom of Big Bertha mingling with the sound of aircraft and the faint thunder of falling bombs, but wasn't afraid. This time her name wasn't on anything, she was sure. Nothing could happen to her now that there was news of Luke.

Ward 6B was like all the others – long and narrow with high windows and a row of iron cots against either wall; lockers between holding water jugs, cups and very little else. The wooden walls had been white-washed, giving the impression that the paint had overflowed on to the beds and the men in them. Whiteness everywhere. Coverlets, bandages, faces, stiffened arms and legs locked in cases of plaster of Paris.

Standing at the head of the ward, Bella looked for Vic but couldn't see him. The strain of the week of waiting, the journey out to this strange little Kentish village and even stranger hospital huts, combined into awful panic with the thought – I can't really remember what he looks like! Why doesn't he wave? Most visitors had already found chairs and were sitting by beds, rustling paper bags, offering hands and kisses.

'Who was it you wanted to see?' asked a passing nurse.

'Sergeant Palmer,' Bella said, and saw him. 'It's all right. He's over there.'

He was at the far end of the ward in a corner and was looking straight at her. She knew of course, why he hadn't waved. She had known all along. Both arms lay at his sides, one encased in plaster, the other heavily bandaged. He was sitting propped up and was smiling. She wondered at his cheerfulness and – imagining herself in the same predicament – decided her face would be as long as a fiddle. Walking swiftly down the aisle, she stopped at the foot of the bed, shyness engulfing her.

His smile stretched to its limit. 'Hello Bella.'

The wretched frog in her throat made her cough before she could answer: 'Hello Vic, how are you?'

'All the better for seeing yo ... sit yourself down.' He nodded to a stool by the bed, laughing a little. 'Well ain't this a turn up! I never really thought yo'd come.'

His unexpected bluntness helped some of the shyness to evaporate and going round the side of the bed she lodged her umbrella against the locker and sat down, asking: 'Whyever not?'

'The distance, and yo not having much spare time.'

She was aware of his gaze roaming over her in a most disconcerting way, as if he were hungry. It created an unexpected disturbing response in her – unwelcome now because it was ill-timed. She had enough on her mind with the question about Luke which was burning her tongue. But it was too soon to blurt it out.

'I gets every Sunday off, and coming into the country makes a real holiday of it.' The cheerfulness of her voice was plainly forced. She wished she was a better actress, and was afraid he too would have heard and taken it as insincerity, which would be all wrong.

His smile had partially faded and was being replaced by a hint of embarrassment as he said: 'Sorry to hear about your Grandad and your brother.'

It was difficult answering. She said: 'Kind of you,' not because he had trodden on a sore place, but because he had said 'brother' rather than 'brothers'. Having to hold back was a kind of mild torture, but she knew she must or he would think she had only come for news of Luke and didn't care twopence for him. She felt annoyed with herself for not being able to handle the situation more easily. All her plans to establish the same friendliness that existed in the letters had got in a tangle. It didn't help to have him staring at her in such a naked way. She tried to think of something pleasant and casual to say, but her brains were in a fog and the words wouldn't come together in any sort of sense. If it hadn't been for her desperate need to know about Luke she might have made some excuse to cut short her visit. But that was impossible as well.

'It's Luke, ain't it? That's why yo've come,' Vic broke the developing silence, jumping over a vast gap of explanations, making final mincemeat of her plan and creating the misunderstanding she had wanted to avoid, out of the truth. Now she would never be able to make him believe that she really was concerned about him and that she considered him her friend. But she wasn't going to start with a lie.

'I dunno that much,' he went on, not waiting for an answer. 'I told Emmie what I'd seen and she was afraid of passing it on to yo in case it was a mistake. She said it wasn't fair to build up hopes that 'ud probably get smashed again, and anyway we couldn't write it in a letter because of it being censored. But me being sent back to Blighty changed things.'

He paused and Bella waited, trying to sit on her monstrous unruly impatience.

'I was a bit dicy at the time. They'd not long carted me back from the front line with this lot,' he looked down at his arms. 'I was raving too ... not all the time, understand. If I had been, then what I saw might've been all part of it.'

She looked at him in despair. He seemed to be wandering in a great circle without getting any nearer to the core. It was like the stories the Admiral used to tell on Sunday nights which went on and on, building up to a peak of tension and hanging there because no amount of begging would make him continue until the next Sunday. She felt like that now, ready to scream, the question pressing hard against her skull.

'We'd been at the front about three days when I clicked,' Vic said just when she thought she must ask him point blank. 'Can't remember too much about it except some of us were doing guard duty by the sap and Fritz was potting at us. Then out of the blue there was this ruddy great crunch and I fell over with me arms feeling as if they was on fire. A long stretch after that when all hell was bustin' ... then the stretcher bearers started rushing about, carrying the lucky ones away and back to base. I was a lucky one, though it didn't feel like it at the time. It was murder that journey. Night and the mud ... well yo don't want to hear about all that. I'll come to the point which was after they'd patched me up at base camp and I'd managed a bit of a kip. We were got ready for another journey, this time to the hospital in Poperinghe. I was loaded on to a stretcher and taken outside, but there was some hold up and the stretcher bearers stood at the back of the ambulance arguing. I wasn't feeling quite so desperate at the time and had me eyes open, and I saw these two blokes in civvies being hustled along by a couple of MPs. They seemed to come out of nowhere and disappear the same way. I suppose it looked like that because I was flat on me back.'

He paused and in her anxiety Bella leaned close to him urging: 'Go on ... please.'

He took a deep breath as if to steady himself. 'I wouldn't have taken much notice in the ordinary way. Yo see some queer sights out there. Prisoners of all sorts and in all kinds of gear. But one of this pair was different, that's why I noticed him. He was brown, like yo only lighter.'

She sat very still, afraid to let the hope go free, telling herself that Luke was not the only man in the British army to have a brown skin. 'Like me just in colour, or really like me?' The answer was immensely important.

'I dunno. It all happened so quick and I didn't get a good look. But come to think of it he was smallish like yo, and there was something in the way he walked ... sort of spring-heeled.' His stare equalled hers in intensity. 'Is it any use?'

The joy, the certainty, wouldn't be restrained any more. She beamed at him. 'Oh yes. It was Luke. I'm sure of it.' Intense happiness was sweeping over her. Luke alive long after the last N–CF inquiries. She wanted to dance and call out to the whole ward: 'He's living ... living ...' The pitch of feeling was so high that before she knew what she was doing she was on her feet and kissing Vic's cheek, saying: 'Thank you, thank you,' then sitting down again, but not embarrassed even then because there was no room in her for anything but delight.

'I could do with a lot of that,' Vic said quietly, his face looking as if he'd come out of a strong wind. 'Yo've caught me at a disadvantage or I'd get it an' all!'

In spite of herself she glanced at his useless arms. His words and manner called out to a part of her that was all confusion. To cover up she said quickly: 'You've got some sauce!' honesty and liking for him making her add: 'But I didn't come just because of Luke you know . . . really I didn't.'

'I'm glad of that.' He smiled again with frank admiration. 'Yo are ever so pretty when yo get excited.'

'Only then?' She dropped into the teasing game for safety.

'Yo're fishing.'

'You started it.'

'That's right.'

She expected him to say more and, when he didn't, sat in silence not knowing what else to say, but it didn't last because he said:

'Yo'll need to have every detail won't yo? Emmie says the N-CF are the people to go to. They'll sort it out. If I wasn't pinned to this bed I'd have half a mind to join 'em and have a go myself at sorting them Army big shots. Bloody lame-brains!'

'You mean you'd be a conchie?' She couldn't believe it.

'Only joking,' but there was enough serious intent behind what he had said to leave her stupefied. He added: 'At least I'm out of the shambles for a while . . . forever if me luck holds.'

'You don't really mean that do you?'

'My right arm's smashed up and my left's all over the place. They ain't going to be usable for a bit.' He leaned back on his pillows and closed his eyes as if the effort of more explanations was beyond him. With his face in repose he looked utterly weary and she reacted with a sudden acute tenderness for him. She reached out and put her hand over the still fingers protruding from the lump of plaster, but they couldn't respond.

He opened his eyes and said: 'Luke was right all along.'

It was as if her world had broken into pieces and reformed. So many old ideas and convictions vanished. The question of what she was doing and why she hadn't joined the women's forces or gone back into making munitions, was suddenly clear. Luke was right! She looked round the ward at the wounded men and their families. Impossible to know if they felt the same, but everyone was heartily sick of the war. There was so much she wanted to say to Vic, so much she wanted to learn about him, but it would have to wait. Already the ward sister was moving from bed to bed, telling everyone it was time for good-byes.

As she stood up she remembered the orange in her pocket and brought it out. 'I meant to give this to you when I first come in, but I forgot. I'll bring another next time, if I can manage to get one. Finding food's like looking for a needle in a haystack!' She put it carefully on top of his locker.

'Yo'll come again, then?' His pleasure was very plain.

'Try and stop me!' She hesitated, then bent over and quickly pecked his cheek for the second time, and found herself kissed in return. As she was buttoning her coat he said:

'It was near Wipers – a place called Dickebusch I saw him. Tell 'em that. And I'll want a full report. Every detail of what happens. I can't write notes ... yet. But I ain't a bad rememberer. We'll find out what them bastards have done with him and make such a stink they'll have to bring him back.'

'Next week then,' she said, touched by his enthusiasm.

'Next week.'

She almost skipped out of the ward, feet flying over the cinder path and out into the lane, thinking of Luke most of all and a little of Catherine and Emily, but resting in the warmth of Vic's genuine concern, and not sparing a thought for her own vanished caution as she began to work out what she must do.

18

'ON yer feet, Sambo.'

Lucas looked blankly at the soldier who had opened the door and was standing square and chunky, looking down on him as he lay on the hard concrete of the floor.

'Y'can get up I suppose? 'Cause if not we'll have to find somethink to make you.'

Lucas struggled to his feet, leaning against the corrugated-iron wall for support. The shackles round his ankles rubbed against his sore skin and he closed his eyes, faintness taking hold.

'Yer luck's in today, Sambo. An audience with Gawd, so get that grub down you and spruce up. There's water and a towel.'

Water? Towel? Lucas opened his eyes again, trying to focus. The narrow cell room, no more than a cupboard, bare of furniture and with only a bucket in one corner and a heap of sacking on which he had been lying, thickened and thinned like a moving fog. He blinked and there was a basin on the floor, a rag beside it, a second basin steaming beside that, a mug behind. His brain – slow and suspicious with uncountable weeks of solitary confinement and only hard biscuits and water to keep him alive – refused to believe what he saw. It was some trick. He wasn't going to drop into another trap. Keep still. Don't say anything.

'Come on, Sambo ... look sharp!' The voice was impatient but not unkind. 'Drink that cocoa. It'll put some heart into you. I ain't going to wait around forever. Ten minutes, that's all yer getting. So if you ain't finished by the time I comes back it's too bad.' The door was pulled to and the bolts shot across.

Slowly Lucas shuffled along the wall, sinking down on to hands and knees as he reached the food. He felt the basin, then the mug behind. They were hot. Quickly he began to drink, gulping the sweet watery liquid, then taking a spoonful of thick lumpy porridge. This was more difficult but he forced some of it down, lubricating it with sips of cocoa. Afterwards he washed as well as he could. He had not been able to shave for a long time and his beard was thick and untrimmed. The unaccustomed feast had made his stomach painful, but already some warmth and a sense of energy were beginning to trickle back. He stood up, still needing the wall for support, but no longer so faint. High up in the curve of the roof, pale blue sky streaked with white cloud was framed in the tiny window lozenge. Staring at it, he tried to remember what month it was. October? Or had they reached November? Days of the week were beyond him. They had become indistinguishable long ago – very soon after he was brought here, which was sometime after they had discovered that his name was Lucas Knight, not Jack Knight. He still didn't understand the confusion. A great black wall stood between the memory of Norman, Stan and himself in a trench together and the next memory of a hospital bed.

The door opened again, letting in light and the same soldier, and cutting short further pondering.

'Stick yer foot out, Sambo, else I can't see to take them irons off.' He knelt down fiddling with key and padlock. 'That's it . . . now then . . . Step out. Yes . . . *out*!' The soldier pushed him along the passage and out of the hut.

Dazed and half-blinded by the unaccustomed brightness, Lucas went uncertainly into the barren autumn world which stretched muddy and cratered to a flat horizon that stunned him with its beauty. It was as if the universe had been divided into two sections. Above, a golden glowing sun cut by stripes of grey cloud which melted into glittering greenish silver. Below lay the raped and ravaged land. Between the two a wood of shattered tree trunks wove sky and earth together in a lacework pattern that took his breath and left him staring.

'Here, Sambo, yer supposed to walk not stand gaping like a

loony. The major don't like to be kept waiting. You don't want to land back in solitary do you?'

A rough shove in the back sent Lucas stumbling forward and he would have fallen if he hadn't caught at the shaft of a cart standing nearby. For the first time he took in his close surroundings. A few corrugated-iron Nissen huts, larger than the one in which he'd been housed, lined a boggy track. A heap of rubble stood on the other side. Perhaps it was not just rubble. It had an entrance out of which a Tommy was climbing. Other Tommies stood round staring . . . staring at *him*.

His particular Tommy gripped his arm, forcing him along towards one of the huts. The effort of staying upright took nearly all his concentration, but he managed to ask: 'What day is it?'

'Bugger me . . . don't yer know that? Saturday. All day!'

They were at the canvas door of the hut and the guard there pushed his head inside. 'Prisoner to see you, Major Russell sir.'

'Bring him in then.'

Lucas found himself standing in front of a table and an officer in mud-stained battle jacket. Nothing was said for several seconds, while a pair of weary grey eyes scrutinized him.

He would not look away. There was not much left except self-respect and to keep that he must never back down, never look away, never give any hint of retreat. But it was hard and he was feeling dizzy again.

'So,' the voice was as weary as the eyes, 'you're the man who will not fight.' There didn't seem to be any answer required and Lucas gave none. The next question was not directed at him, but at the Tommy who'd come with him. 'Fit to travel is he, Corporal Mott?'

'Seems all right, sir. He can walk.'

'Has he been given breakfast?'

'Yessir.'

'Eaten it?'

'Yessir.'

'Right. Take him to the transport wagon, Corporal. Sergeant Newman has been given the details. See him. And, Corporal . . .'

'Yessir?'

'Don't let the prisoner do anything silly. They expect him back in one piece. God knows why, but they do.'

'Yessir. Prisoner, about turn . . . quick march!'

But Lucas, unable to bear the winding suspense any longer, stayed where he was, words bursting from him: 'Where is it? Where am I going?'

Corporal Mott looked at him in shocked surprise. 'Here, watch it yer . . .'

'All right, Corporal. He's entitled to know.'

Entitled? – Lucas thought. *Entitled!* His ears must be playing tricks, hearing the merest suspicion of admiration.

'You are being returned to England. What they propose to do with you when you get there I don't know. Now, get going!'

This time the interview was definitely at an end and Lucas went out into the singing sunshine. England! Blighty! He was going home.

Outside the grim blackened frontage of Wandsworth prison a small breeze stirred the dank November morning air. Bella shrank into her clothes and Vic slipped his arm round her shoulders.

'Nice I can do that. Wait till me other arm's as good!'

'I ain't cold.' Bella glanced at his right arm which hung in a sling, her smile dissolving into a yawn. 'It's the waiting.'

'I knows that. Wouldn't yo rather sit in the motor car?' He looked back at the battered Model T Ford and Catherine Ashe who was in the driving seat.

Bella shook her head. 'It's better out here. Better for her too. She's a saint offering to come. I dunno how we'd manage if she hadn't. Luke must be pretty bad or they wouldn't be letting him out of jug.'

'He's alive and that's what counts.'

'Norman ain't.'

'Yo don't know that. There was no news of Luke for months and he's turned up.'

She shrugged. 'P'raps yer right.'

'I knows I'm right.'

'Cocky!' She gave him a nudge, adding: 'But it's real queer the way there was all them months of nothink, then after I'd told Catherine what you'd seen everythink seemed to get going all at once.'

'Yo calls nine months of waiting all at once? Funny sense of time yo've got.'

'I means all them letters and telegrams and having to see that Government bloke.'

'That really stirred things. I liked that! Proves my point about never giving up.' He sounded smugly pleased.

Bella leaned her head briefly against his cheek. 'Yer such a comfort. Never look on the black side.'

He gave her a small squeeze. 'That's just what I do. All the time.'

She was on the defensive straight away, saw him grinning and relaxed as much as she could with a rueful smile.

He tweaked her ear. 'One up to me! Bit of a fighting cock underneath ain't yo?'

'Hen.'

'Spring chick. I wouldn't be fancying an old boiler.'

If the tautness of waiting hadn't been there she would have laughed. Part of her was warmed and cosseted by his fun and his presence. His good humour showed more often now, though there were still frightening times when he seemed to go away into himself, refusing to speak and staring fixedly at things she couldn't see. The memory of the last time that had happened brought another cold shudder, and now when the sudden sound of maroons gatecrashed on her thoughts she almost leapt in the air, pressing against him and thinking – not today ... not another raid! The grip on her shoulder was like a vice and she could feel him trembling. There was nothing in the sky, nor any sound of aero-engines, yet the maroons thundered on. Catherine was out of the car staring round. In the road traffic had slowed to a halt. People were climbing from a bus and beginning to come from buildings. Everyone was gazing about, bewildered. Near to the Ford car an old man clambered painfully from a totters cart. When he reached the ground Bella saw him raise both arms in the air and begin to jig about shouting. The words reached across to her:

'It's over . . . the bloody war's finished! We've won!'

Vic breathed: 'My God!' then shouted at Bella: 'They said it would happen soon. It's the Armistice . . . the bloody Armistice. It's really come. Christ Almighty!' hugging her to him, not caring about his damaged arm.

She came out of his embrace, pulling back, scarcely able to realize what he was saying or what was happening, and turned towards the great studded doors. A sense of unreality seized her along with an awful fear that the growing pandemonium would prevent the small door from ever opening. But already it was ajar. She couldn't move. Could hardly breathe as she focused with all of her being on the uniformed warder who emerged first, then on the thin brown figure who followed with a slight stagger. The warder said something which she didn't catch and Luke answered.

'Go on,' Vic gave her a gentle shove, breaking the spell. 'What are yo waiting for? The poor bloke looks as if he could do with a bit of help.'

Standing outside the prison which had housed him for the past fortnight, Lucas looked at Freedom. It didn't matter that everything was smudged and not quite stable, or that his body was aching and boneless. He'd been unshackled and was once again part of the boundless world. With sudden insight he seemed to step back over the years and feel as Midnight must have felt. It was as if they were one. Slaves and now free. The moment passed and he drank in great gulps of glorious intoxicating damp London air, seeing Bella walking towards him.

'What a way to celebrate yer release, mate.' The warder was all smiles. 'That row means the war's over.'

'Over?' The word meant very little.

'Yes, over. So go and enjoy yerself. With a bit of luck they won't want you back inside again. You deserve a break.'

The hint was wasted on Lucas, but Bella heard. She came very close, putting her arms round him and whispering so that only he could hear: 'It *is* over – whatever they says. I won't never let you go back . . . *never*!'

The well-remembered fierce protectiveness in her voice made him smile. It occurred to him that this was the first smile he had managed in a long time. He said:

'We did it, Bel. We won.'

She let go enough to be able to see his face. '*You* won. I dunno about the rest of us.'

The weakness he had been fending off took over. He swayed and felt Bella clutch him. There was someone else as well. A soldier supporting him on the other side, helping him towards a motor car where a woman with a gaunt face which reminded him of someone he couldn't recall was waiting. Somehow he got into the car, collapsing against the leather seat, closing his eyes. He heard Bella say:

'He's all right, Catherine. You can start up,' and felt the car chunter into life. As they moved away down the road and began the long journey home, the weakness slowly subsided and as they were leaving Lambeth Bridge he opened his eyes, recognizing the place immediately. With a rush of excitement he leaned forward, asking:

'Can you drive us up Millbank?'

'The traffic will be thick,' Catherine warned.

'Well just try it, please.' His anticipation was intense.

'We'll be all day.' Bella sounded anxious.

Lucas took her hand. 'It don't matter. We've got all day.' He wanted to reassure her; talk to her and tell her everything he'd thought during the long prison months, but now was not the right moment. He relaxed back against the seat again, watching people like ants pouring out to swarm on humid days. They crowded the pavements and spilled over into the road as they joined hands dancing. The lowing of ships came from the river to mingle with the sound of car hooters, police whistles, cheering and shouts. A scout on a bicycle passed within touching distance, blowing a bugle as he wove in and out of the crammed vehicles. It was wonderful chaos, and above a serene sky was crossed by a line of birds. He smelled soot and petrol and horses, and determined to hold everything sharp in his mind. That was the way to grow.

Slowly they crawled up Millbank until they reached Old Palace Yard where the traffic jammed to a halt, and with the same stunning perfect vibrant clarity he saw the statue in just the same way he had that first time so many years ago. The crowned man astride his stepping horse, arm and sword raised aloft. Richard the Lionheart – a huge strong triumphant bronze mass poised on a decorated pedestal, round which a string of people were dancing. It seemed appropriate. He gazed at it, feeling the same urge to touch and experience the powerful muscular shapes with his hands, and knew with certain joy that all the horrors of war had left that first sure conviction untouched. This was what he wanted to do. From now on this was what he *would* do. Nobody and no thing was going to change that.

'Looks as if we're stuck good and proper,' Bella said, breaking in on his thoughts.

He smiled at her with complete satisfaction. 'Who cares? We've all the time in the world.'

Also in Puffin Plus

BASKETBALL GAME

Julius Lester

Allen is black and Rebecca is white, and in Nashville, Tennessee, in 1956, that means they must keep apart. They like each other, they're interested in each other, but is that enough to survive the deeply rooted prejudice that surrounds them? A moving, truthful book that captures the tenderness of young love but also its helplessness in the face of adult hostility.

THE WRITING ON THE WALL

Lynne Reid Banks

Kev is a bad influence – or at least that's what Tracy's dad thinks – so she isn't surprised when her parents won't let her go on holiday with him alone. But Tracy is determined to have some fun before she has to settle down in a boring job, like her sister. So she finds a good way of getting round her dad – at least it seems a good way at the time . . .